Hangman's Lane

It seems brutally unjust that it should be Constable Wardle who finds his wife's murdered body down Hangman's Lane. But then the whole case is a mess, from the general failure to notify the right people at the right moment to the traffic accident forcing the detective in charge into early retirement. It is thirteen weeks later when Chief Inspector Lyle arrives in Grantley, seconded from another force to reopen the inquiry. By then even a slim chance of discovering convenient forensic evidence – fingerprints, footprints, the odd stray hair – has disappeared.

What Lyle finds is a close community eager to discuss the late Tabitha Wardle's extra-marital activities but struck dumb at the suggestion that any one of their member could kill. Lyle is forced to rely on his genuine understanding of human nature to prove them wrong. And all the time the murderer is likely to kill again.

Complex and compulsive, highlighting the uncomfortable fact that we are all capable of murder, *Hangman's Lane* is a first class police procedural by the master of the genre.

HANGMAN'S LANE

JOHN WAINWRIGHT

LITTLE, BROWN AND COMPANY

A *Little, Brown* Book

First published in Great Britain in 1992 by
Little, Brown and Company

Copyright © 1992 by John and Avis Wainwright

The right of John Wainwright to be identified as
author of this work has been asserted by him in
accordance with the Copyright, Designs and Patents Act 1988.

A CIP catalogue record for this book is available
from the British Library.

ISBN 0 356 20567 3

Photoset in North Wales by
Derek Doyle & Associates, Mold, Clwyd.
Printed and bound in Great Britain by
Mackays of Chatham PLC, Chatham, Kent

Little, Brown and Company (UK) Limited
165 Great Dover Street
London SE1 4YA

Hangman's Lane

PART ONE
The Killing – Hunt's Case

TUESDAY, July 31st

11.55 p.m.

Wardle climbed from the van, stretched and gazed up at the night sky. He was tired, but not too tired to appreciate the cool beauty after a hot and sticky day. Wardle fancied himself as a bit of a literary gent; he toyed around in his brain trying to find flash phrases with which to describe the midnight heavens. 'The three-quarters moon swam around, beyond clouds which resembled tar streaks against a navy-blue back-cloth.' Very nice. Very poetic. Maybe slightly purple at the edges, but what the hell? Anyway, he was tired. Ten-to-six night-shift, last night, covering 'A' Beat at Easedale. Court Duty this morning – the dirty sod who'd been flashing his chopper along Hangman's Lane, up here on Gauntley Beat, six months suspended . . . and not a minute more than the animal had deserved. Then a couple of hours' catnap in an armchair, before coming on duty at 2.00 p.m. until 6.00 p.m. Then a meal and out again at 10.00 p.m. and (hopefully) off duty at 2.00 a.m. and into bed, between cool, sweet-smelling sheets.

And, boy, was he ready for it.

His tiredness made silly, illogical things annoy him. The telephone kiosk along whose side he waited. Why one of the all-glass monstrosities? Why not one of the old-fashioned, small-paned, scarlet-painted landmarks the British public had long grown used to? From a police point of view – from the point of view of coppers who were

3

required to hang around telephone kiosks waiting for messages from some soft-numbered colleague who was required to pass bad news down the line, the old-time kiosks were cosy. On a wild, wet and windy night they seemed to give more than mere shelter. They were snug, box-like womb-substitutes. They were solidly built and, for a few minutes, they were almost a tiny, comfortable room. But not these. These weren't even greenhouses. In weather like it had been that day, they were like Perspex ovens. In rough weather they gave shelter enough, but at the same time they allowed a complete, all-round view of what was going on outside.

Anyway, it wasn't necessary. Hanging around a telephone kiosk for the best part of a quarter-of-an-hour went out with police whistles. Personal radios – walkie-talkies – had stopped all that rubbish. And if, like Gauntley, the beat was way and gone to hell beyond the limited range of walkie-talkie reception, the radio van was there to provide the answer.

An old ex-Z-car vehicle. Before Z-Cars became old hat and a new policing gimmick took its place. Like this old Morris van that went with the beat . . . and thank God for small mercies. Once upon a time it had been a bicycle beat, and *that* would have taken the silly grin off the monkey's face. Gauntley Beat by pedal cycle. Christ, some of those old-time coppers must have had leg muscles like steel hawsers.

A one-time-Z-car vehicle, complete with radio, but Percy insisted upon making a full ten-minute 'point' at a telephone kiosk half-way through a four-hour shift.

'Safer,' he'd insisted. 'More confidential.'

'I don't see that.' Wardle had raised token objection.

'Radio waves can be intercepted.'

'Only if you know the wavelength.'

'Wardle.' Percy had switched to his weary-of-a-never-ending-line-of-dumb-coppers tone. 'People listen in. A modern radio – even a *cheap* radio – can pick up police transmissions. People get a kick.'

'Some kick.'

4

'They think they're listening to something they shouldn't hear.'

'They *are*.'

'A sort of Peeping Tom thrill.'

'Voyeurism?'

'Exactly.'

'Does it matter?'

'It *could* matter. Something we really *don't* want non-police personnel to hear.'

'Oh, my word, "Non-police personnel".'

'Constable Wardle.' Percy's tone had hardened. He was pushing rank, as far as anybody not too sure of his ability to exercise authority *could* push rank. A mite pompously, he continued, 'This is not a subject for debate. Quite simply, it is *my* decision. You will make an appointment at one of the telephone kiosks on your beat, at least once in every four hours of duty.'

That was Percy, and it was as well to know him; know how far he could be pushed. And the poor, miserable bugger couldn't tolerate opposition – or even much argument – from lower ranks without fizzing somebody.

No hardship, of course. Parking the van at the kiosk at Calvert's Corner was no more onerous than driving the bloody thing along the lanes of the beat. Merely unnecessary. Merely a minor limitation upon the freedom of motion throughout the beat and thus (perhaps) making for a less than absolute discouragement of the tiny lawlessnesses which punctuated the gentle progression of this very reasonable and well-behaved community.

Ah well, not to worry.

There was a momentary stillness. A sudden absence of sound – even the accumulation of tiny, wildlife sounds of the countryside – like a lull in a conversation. Like a hole in a great garment of soft noise. Then with equal suddenness, beyond Calvert's village store, beyond the tarmac apron of the store upon which stood the telephone kiosk, a dog fox barked. Maybe half a mile away. Maybe more. The old boy was cross about something. It was there in the quick snap of his bark. A complaint about the hot discomfort of the past day, perhaps. A rabbit that had found the safety of its burrow. A scent that had petered out.

Wardle gave a quick, half-smile. Gauntley Beat. His own personal area of responsibility . . . and it was like this. A place of grass and trees, of farms and woods and wildlife. A place where a dog fox had the freedom to voice his complaint about something to an almost-full moon.

The kiosk's phone bell rang, Wardle opened the door, answered the call and recognised Tommy Boyle's voice.

'Percy says hang on there. He's coming out.'

'Will do.'

'All quiet, old mate?'

'Quiet,' agreed Wardle. 'It wants to stay that way until two.'

Midnight

'Percy', of whom a lot was being thought and a little said, was driving his motor car beyond the outskirts of Easedale township. He left the street lighting behind and headed up the slope towards the Pennine foothills and the outside beat of Gauntley. The headlamps pushed a fan of light ahead of the car, and the cat's eyes switched themselves on and off as if by magic.

'Percy'. Police Sergeant 1018 Percival Horace Poole, section sergeant at Easedale Police Section, Beechwood Brook Division of the county constabulary. He was a man who held infinite opinions and suffered almost as many fears.

The seat of his present worry was his guts. Some weeks ago, his medic had diagnosed diverticulitis but – partly because he had never before heard of the ailment – Poole had serious doubts. The doubts had been intensified by the medic's throwaway remark, 'I have a friend. A surgeon. Would you like to see him?' Poole had declined the offer but, as of that moment, he'd been quite sure. Ulcers? Well, if he was lucky – very lucky – it might only be

6

ulcers. But the chances were, given *his* luck, it was something else. Cancer. Cancer of the stomach. Gut cancer . . . he'd be happy to lay money on it.

Which was why throughout his waking life and regardless of whatever else he was doing part of his mind was (figuratively speaking) groping around in his stomach. At the moment, somewhere down in his innards, a pain was about to come to life. He knew it. He could sense it. And, moreover, it was due to stab him just where the seat belt crossed his lower abdomen. Just where that damned medic drove stiffened fingers about three inches deep.

Poole removed a hand from the wheel long enough to ease the pressure of the seat belt. He decided that next time he visited his GP he'd be very firm. No more pushing in of fingers. The man knew where it hurt. His job was to ease pain . . . not aggravate it.

WEDNESDAY, August 1st

12.10 a.m.

A new day. It felt no different. It looked no different. But it *was* a new day; fresh from the calendar and touched by only ten minutes of time. Indeed, a new month. And if the forecasters were to be believed, the new month was going to start just as hot and just as sticky as the old month had ended. Not much difference, then ... but Wardle knew that, back at home, Tabs and Madge would have solemnly said 'Hares' in unison, just before midnight then, with equal solemnity, would have both said 'White rabbits' immediately after midnight. And had he been at home he, too, would have had to join in the monthly ritual.

But he wasn't at home, so he yawned and wished he *was* at home.

He yearned for a cigarette, but he knew he hadn't got any, and he hadn't got any because, a week back, he'd stopped smoking. That's why he longed for a cigarette. That, and because of the time, and because he hadn't slept for far too long. A cigarette would have helped ... but he'd stopped smoking.

He muttered, 'Sod it to hell,' then started drawing in deep breaths of moderately cool night air, but it didn't help. He was still taking deep breaths, and feeling no better for it, when Poole arrived.

Poole climbed from his car, jerking his head in a single nod, then asked the question all 'visiting' sergeants ask of patrolling constables.

'All quiet?'

'Quiet,' said Wardle.

'What happened this morning?'

'Boothroyd?'

'The Indecent Exposure clown. Convicted?'

'Of course.' Wardle sounded surprised that the question was necessary. 'Six months, suspended.'

'Good. No more than he deserves.'

It was an exchange – a conversation – but it was a strictly small-hours-of-the-morning, police conversation. No animation. Questions asked, with no apparent interest in the answers. And gaps – unnaturally long silences – between each sentence.

Poole's open palm rested lightly on the side of his stomach.

Wardle asked, 'Digestion still troubling you?'

'Something,' grunted Poole.

'It goes with the job,' observed Wardle.

'What?'

'Indigestion. Ulcers. Meals at all hours. No set sleep pattern. It's bound to get you, in time.'

'Maybe.' Poole turned, bent forward and took the keys from the ignition of his car. As he locked the car doors, he said, 'I'll give you a company visit. We'll use the van. Boyle knows I'm out with you. If he wants me, he can reach me by radio.' As he slipped the keys into his trouser pocket, he added, 'A nice night. A few lungfuls of country air won't come amiss.'

12.35 a.m.

Wardle dropped down to second and turned the van into the mouth of Hangman's Lane.

He said, 'Boothroyd's battlefield.'

'Uhuh.'

'It's also where some of the local Lotharios park, for a humping session.'

'You check?' Poole sounded mildly disapproving.

'That the females are over age, and that nobody's

9

committing obvious rape.'

'Ah!' Poole nodded a slightly late understanding.

Wardle said, 'I doubt if there'll be anybody here at this time. Tuesday. Maybe on a Saturday night, but it's work tomorrow.'

Poole grunted agreement, then leaned forward to peer through the windscreen and along the path of the van's headlights.

There is a Hangman's Lane – or its equivalent – in almost every village. It was a U-shaped lane which led nowhere, which merely left the B-class road then re-joined it about half a mile farther along. Nobody lived on Hangman's Lane. Its purpose – its sole purpose – was to allow farmers and farm-workers to reach fields and woods well away from the road. Its average width was about fifteen feet, and its surface was hard-packed earth covered in stunted grass over which the council spread a thin carpet of granite chippings. It was an ideal surface for the wheels of farm machinery, but motor cars were wise to keep their speed down to a level which didn't flick the chippings up onto their bodywork.

Every so often, gates led from the lane into the adjoining fields. The hedges, on both sides of the lane, were of hawthorn, blackthorn with, occasionally, the glossy leaves of a holly bush. Trees – sycamores, willows and a few stunted elms – elbowed their way into the hedge, like obese belly-dancers in a line of trim chorus girls. And, of course, wild-life was there. Rabbits, stoats, hedgehogs, weasels, mice, rats, voles, moles, a regular hunt of marauding cats and an occasional inquisitive dog. Hangman's Lane, its hedges and the adjoining fields was a tiny but bloody battlefield. Amateur naturalists and botanists loved to wander its length and kid themselves that nature was a pure and childish thing, but remained deliberately unaware of the never-ending blood-letting and carnage which went on at ankle level.

Wardle braked the van to a halt as the headlights illuminated a gate left ajar.

He said, 'Bloody walkers. They always leave signs of their passing.'

10

'I'll close it.' Poole was opening the van door as he spoke. He walked to the gate and, despite the light from the van's headlamps, he carried a three-battery torch, which he switched on as he neared the open gate. The beam from the torch was like a miniature searchlight and as he grasped the top bar of the gate he swept the beam across the grass of the field and along the back of the hedgerow.

He stopped the beam, froze and breathed, 'Holy cow!'

Wardle saw the expression on the beat sergeant's face and through the wound-down window called, 'Something wrong?'

'You . . .' Poole swallowed. 'You can say that.'

Wardle switched off the engine and climbed from the van. He, too, had a torch and as he joined Poole he sent its beam towards the spot where the other beam ended.

The increased illumination made her look even worse. She was on her back, with her face turned away from them. Her dress had once been of a patterned blue material. Now, from the waist up, it was glistening scarlet . . . what there was left of it. Much of it was missing and a great, cave-like hole exposed the contents of the chest cavity. She was dead – she couldn't *possibly* be alive – and the grass around her sprawling body was well stained with what had once flowed through her veins.

Wardle said, 'Christ Almighty!'

'She – she can't be alive.' Poole seemed to have difficulty in keeping his voice steady.

'No.' It was a quick, soft, snapped-off agreement.

'But, y'know . . . she might be.'

'She's not alive,' muttered Wardle. 'God Almighty, man. She *can't* be.'

'She *might* be.' The rising panic was there in the hint of a quaver in Poole's tone. 'She might be,' he repeated. Then, 'We have to find out. You're the expert.'

'Look, we shouldn't go near till—'

'You're the expert.' Poole's voice was pitched a little high. 'All that First Aid. All those cups and such. You go. Check she is dead.'

'Dammit, sergeant, we shouldn't. We're all trained to

11

keep the scene of—'

'Do it, Wardle. She might be alive. All right, it's an order . . . just check.'

For a moment Wardle hesitated. The truth was, he didn't want to go near the dead woman. And she was dead. Nothing surer. And what Poole was saying about First Aid wasn't really relevant. She was *dead* . . . well beyond First Aid. Anyway, all that tooling around with triangular bandages and pressure points in a classroom or in a competition hall wasn't the same. It wasn't like this. There wasn't the muck and the guts and the blood. It wasn't like this at all . . .

'Check,' insisted Poole. 'Don't worry. I'll carry the can. But one of us has to make sure before we do anything else. And you're the expert.'

Slowly – reluctantly – Wardle made his way across the close-cropped grass. He walked carefully and checked where he put his feet. He reached the woman and squatted down on his heels. Hesitantly – carefully – he put out a hand and eased the face away from the covering of grass and leaves. For a moment the world seemed to halt on its axis; Poole would later swear that there was a distinct silence before Wardle raised his head and mouthed words, without speaking.

'What?' Poole stared across at the bloodless face and the gaping eyes.

Wardle opened and closed his mouth, but the words wouldn't come.

'Eh? I can't hear you.'

'T-T-Tabs.' His jaw muscles and his throat muscles seemed to strain to near breaking-point before he was able to force the word out. Then, in a gradually strengthening voice, which rose to something like the scream of a wounded animal, 'It's – it's Tabs. It's my wife, Tabs. It's *Tabs!'*

3.30 a.m.

It had taken the first hour to kick-start the machine into life. The Met, a handful of the larger police forces and some of the old-time major constabularies handled murder as an almost daily occurrence, but not the Calfordshire County force. Sure there'd been other murders; other murders that same year. Indeed – and being cold-bloodedly statistical – this was the twenty-second murder of the year and the year was already past the half-way stage. Twenty-two murders in seven months equated with a remarkably law-abiding society. Less than one a week . . . and few of them needing even token 'detection'. In the main, cosy little family killings. Man-and-wife jobs. Carving-knife or coal-hammer situations, with the culprit just as obvious as the corpse. Run-of-the-mill stuff in which the CID strolled to centre-stage, collected undeserved kudos then retired into obscurity to watch TV cops demonstrate exactly how it should be done.

But not this one.

It had taken Poole almost fifteen minutes to quieten Wardle, and the sheer stunning effect of the shock had, eventually, helped enough to dumb the constable into a semi-coma of complete non-understanding.

Then, trying to control his own shaking frame, Poole had radioed in and tried to be methodical.

'Gauntley Beat to Headquarters Radio Room. This is Police Sergeant Poole here. I need urgent assistance, please.'

The voice of a snooty policewoman had replied, 'Radio Room to Gauntley Beat. Accepted radio procedure should be used on all transmissions, please. Over.'

'Police Sergeant Poole here. I am at the scene of a major crime. I need assistance, urgently. Over.'

'What assistance. Over.'

'I need an ambulance, immediately, for an officer. Then I need Motor Patrol units. At least two. Then I require Inspector Mantell of Beechwood Brook Division to be

13

informed of my location and requested to join me.'

'What is your location, Gauntley Beat?'

'I am Sergeant Poole and I am at Gauntley Beat. Exact location Hangman's Lane. And please treat this message as urgent.'

It had been all wrong; the 'over-to-you', 'Roger-and-out' crap had been flushed straight down the tube. But it had done the trick. Poole's near-panic had transmitted itself over the air waves and things had started happening.

Within fifteen minutes the first squad car nosed its way down Hangman's Lane and a couple of motor patrol men were there to lend a willing hand. Within the next five minutes the ambulance arrived and Wardle was wrapped in a warm blanket to counter the shock, then loaded onto a stretcher and into the ambulance and away.

The older motor patrol officer had asked, 'Is it too much for him then?'

'Just about too much for *anybody*.' With the arrival of other officers, Poole had regained some of his own composure. He'd added, 'The woman out there on the grass is Wardle's wife.'

'Wardle?'

'The constable they've just taken away.'

'Hell's teeth! That is *rough*.'

Ten minutes later a second squad car had joined them, and a firm wireless communication between Hangman's Lane and the Radio Room at force headquarters had been established. There was a link between Gauntley Beat and the rest of the world. A lifeline. A means of screaming for help if necessary.

At 1.15 a.m. Mantell and a third squad car had joined the growing 'police presence'. Gradually, there was a gentle relaxing of the impossible tension. There was an acceptance of an originally frightening fact; that out there, in the rural tranquillity of Gauntley Beat, one of the top crimes in the calendar had been committed.

It is possible that the presence of Mantell had brought about the change of attitude.

Police Inspector Harold Mantell. One of those men

14

never meant to be a police officer; a man who as a beat copper had made a ten-course meal of a fiddling road traffic offence; a nuisance to his colleagues and an embarrassment to his senior officers. So they'd made him a sergeant and, in so doing, had done little to lessen his nuisance value, nor yet to make him less of an embarrassment.

Then somebody had said, 'Make the clown into an inspector. The sergeants will prevent him from going too mad, and his super should be able to hide him away somewhere.'

And as a uniformed divisional inspector Mantell had prospered.

Mantell had known what had to be done. Any and every situation, he'd known the sequence and the priorities. He'd read them and learned them by rote. On paper, he was a cracker. Since early in his service he'd known exactly what to do. His downfall had always been his complete inability to execute these things. In a strange and peculiar way, he was ham-handed when it came to practical policing.

But that was quite all right once he'd made inspector. Now he was merely required to tell other people what to do . . . *they* put the theories into practice.

Therefore when Mantell arrived and took over from Poole, things had looked up a little.

He'd stood at the gate, examined the corpse in the beams from torches and asked, 'Somebody's checked she's dead, I take it?'

'We – er – we think so.' Poole knew he'd dropped one, but tried to pick up as much as possible. 'Wardle would have said. If there'd been any doubt, he'd . . .'

Mantell had murmured, 'Not a qualified medical practitioner?'

'Well, er . . .'

'And in a state of shock.'

'Yes, sir. But . . .'

'We need an MD. We've nothing until she's been certified as dead.'

15

It had been 'The Book', and Mantell was a whizz-kid as far as 'The Book' was concerned. As, for example, when he'd asked about the CID.

'I – er – I was going to let them know.' Poole had realised that he'd dropped another moderate-sized clanger. 'I was, y'know . . . I had Wardle to see to, sir.'

Mantell had motioned one of the squad car officers nearer.

'Another radio message please, constable. Ask them to notify Detective Inspector Eccles of Beechwood Brook Division. And ask them to tell him that we haven't – have *not* – yet notified Detective Sergeant Moody.'

Then Mantell had organised the actual scene of the crime . . . the 'suspected crime' as he insisted upon calling it.

A motor patrol officer at each end of Hangman's Lane.

'Nobody – other than our own officers – allowed beyond that point. We haven't yet any tape to make a proper barrier. But the thing to remember: it looks like a crime and, if it turns out to *be* a crime, there'll be a search required. As clean as possible for the search detail . . . right?'

When the medic had arrived Mantell had been almost old-maidish in his fussy detail.

'Now, doctor, I'd like you to cross the grass and examine the woman.'

'That's why I'm here, I presume.'

'Quite, but you must disturb things as little as possible. Don't move her. Merely check that she's no longer alive. Then we know where we stand.'

'She's as dead as last week's mutton. I can see that from here.'

'Ah, yes, but we have to have a qualified medical practitioner to certify her dead, before we can . . .'

'Inspector.' The medic had met Mantell before. 'She's dead. Kaput. Gone to meet her Maker. I'll stroll across and feel her pulse if that makes you happy. But it won't make her any less dead.'

'A rough estimate of the time, perhaps?' Mantell had suggested.

16

'Time of death?'

'If you could, please.'

'I can't.'

'Eh?'

'Mantell, old son, you've been reading too many Agatha Christies. Outside. Wildly varying temperatures. This weather. Out there on the grass. Not to mention what she ate last, and when she ate it. What she's wearing.'

'Oh.'

'Unless you're prepared to let me stick a thermometer up her bum—'

'I'm not.'

'—it's not much good. It wouldn't be much good *then*. A quick PM might do the trick. As far as I'm concerned, if she isn't going off she's snuffed it within the last few hours.'

'Rigor mortis?' Mantell had looked very worried.

'They tell me.' The medic had nodded. 'But the text books can't make up their respective minds. Anyway, there's an almost immediate stiffening in certain violent deaths. You pay your money, you take your pick. It tends to flummox everybody.'

Nevertheless, when he'd returned from a quick examination of the body, the medic had looked more serious, and had said, 'It's a shotgun wound. From fairly close range at a guess. She didn't suffer. She didn't have *time* to suffer.'

The remark had set the pace.

Mantell had said, 'An Unlawful Killing. I think we can take that for granted now.'

Detective Inspector Eccles and Detective Sergeant Moody had arrived together. In Moody's car.

Moody had said, 'They notified me from Headquarters.'

Eccles had added, 'No point in cluttering the place up with more cars than necessary.'

Poole had taken them to the gate and had then shone a torch beam onto the dead woman.

'Dead?' Eccles had asked. It had been merely a formal question.

'Certified.'

'Good. Do we know who she is?'

17

'Tabitha Wardle.'

'Wardle? That's the same name as—'

'It's his wife.'

'Jesus!'

'He found her . . . in effect.'

'Hell's teeth!' The Detective Inspector had pursed his lips into a whistle, and had then said, 'You were there at the time?'

'I was here. Where I'm now standing.'

'Good,' Eccles had nodded his satisfaction. He'd continued, 'You'll be anchor man then.'

'Eh?'

'Make your pocket book up, Sergeant. Show yourself finding her . . . we don't want to upset Wardle more then we have to. Then stick around. Go with the body to the morgue. Be at the post-mortem. Give evidence at the inquest. Then see her buried. Be in the background at the funeral.'

'I – er – I don't see . . .'

'The same body, Sergeant. The *same* body. In effect, it's in your custody, until it's buried.'

'Oh!'

'It has been known . . . That's your main job. To make bloody sure it isn't done this time.'

And that was about it. Until dawn – until the sun rose high enough to give some decent light – it was a matter of standing around, making sure nothing was disturbed and getting ready for the rush of activity – supposing there *was* a rush of activity – which would arrive with daylight.

Mantell returned to Beechwood Brook Divisional Headquarters, there to arrange for another section sergeant – Backhouse – to take over from Poole, while Poole was busy corpse-watching. He also robbed Peter and paid Paul, until he had enough spare coppers to take over the grassroots work, come six o'clock.

And after much soul-searching and a great deal of hesitation, Eccles decided to notify Detective Chief Superintendent Hunt that an unlawful killing – suspected murder – had been committed within the boundaries of the force.

18

*

Detective Chief Superintendent Septimus Hunt was having a high old time. He had this old chest of drawers; scratched, battered and all in all, in a God-awful condition. But that didn't matter, because every drawer was stuffed solid with beautiful bank notes. Enough money to see him clear, and in luxury, for the rest of his life. More than enough . . . and every last penny was his.

If, that was, he could wrestle it up the stairs and into the third-floor flat he'd come to live in. And getting it up those stairs wasn't easy. Especially with Ethel, his daughter-in-law, dressed in a loose-fitting bikini, sitting on top of the drawers; grinning down at him. Ethel was being her usual prattish self. She wouldn't shift. She wouldn't accept the fact that, with one tit adrift from its cup, she didn't look in the least exotic. She looked repulsive. And (worst of all) she wouldn't stop ringing that bloody bicycle bell.

Gradually, Hunt surfaced from sleep and shook aside the dream, but the bell continued ringing. Not a bicycle bell, the telephone bell.

He stretched out an arm, lifted the receiver and said, 'Hunt.'

'Sir.' Hunt recognised the slightly distorted voice of Detective Inspector Eccles. 'I think we have a murder on our hands.'

'Murder?'

'Beechwood Brook Division.'

'Where?'

'Easedale Section. Gauntley Beat.'

'Details.' Suddenly Hunt was very wide awake. He hoisted himself into a sitting position, and continued, 'A quick run-down of what's happened, what's been done so far and who's in attendance.'

'A woman called Tabitha Wardle, blasted in the chest with a shotgun. She's the wife of the village bobby.'

'Wardle?'

'Constable Wardle. He found the body.'

'And take that with a pinch of salt,' growled Hunt. 'Keep

19

him on ice, till I arrive.'

'He's in hospital, recovering from shock.'

'Make sure he stays there. And no questions till I've had a go at him.'

'Understood, sir.'

'Go on.'

'A field off Hangman's Lane. A country lane – no houses, no buildings – just a lane leading to field openings, then back to the road again. Everything's cordoned off, as far as we're able. I've stationed . . .'

'What's "as far as we're able" mean?'

'It's cordoned off, sir.'

'Tight?'

'Yes, sir.' But Eccles's voice didn't carry complete certainty.

'Inspector, I want it *cordoned*. I don't want so much as a mouse to get past without being checked. I shall be out there within the next hour, and any slap-happy policing and I'll have somebody's balls in the meat grinder.'

Madge Wardle stared from the window of the police house and wished, with all her heart, that either Tabs or Alex would come home. She was sixteen years old, she'd enjoyed a good education, she knew exactly how many beans made five and she'd long since clocked the late-night, TV horror films as a means of getting rid of a surplus of tomato ketchup.

Nevertheless . . .

Sam Cooley, for instance. Sam Cooley made believe he was a small-time chicken farmer. Not so. Sam Cooley was a moderately big-time shop-breaker, office-breaker and safe-cracker. The chicken farming was meant to be a cover, but it wasn't much of a cover. Most of Gauntley knew exactly what Sam Cooley's game was. Certainly Alex knew and, one day, Alex wouldn't be able to turn his usual blind eye. Then . . .

Then there'd be trouble. Big, *big* trouble.

The truth was, Alex wasn't a great copper. He wasn't even a good copper. But he was a very honest copper. If a thing sat up and spat him in the eye, he wouldn't pretend it hadn't happened. In his own bumbling, cack-handed way,

20

he'd *do* something.

Which would make Sam Cooley cross, and when Sam Cooley lost his temper . . .

Alex could be lying under a hedge somewhere with the back of his head caved in. He could be in the Emergency Ward of the Mark Cullpepper Hospital. He really could. Something very terrible could have happened to Alex, because he was that sort of a mutt.

As *for* Tabs . . .

Tabs was ill. Nor was it an illness for which medicine could be prescribed. Nevertheless, she *was* ill, and Alex knew it, and Alex made allowances.

Even so she shouldn't be out until this time. She was never out until this time. Correction: never had she been out until this time in the past. But unpredictability was part of the illness. So who knew? Who could guess?

Madge Wardle was a very modern miss. She called her parents by their Christian names and gave little thought to that habit. Nevertheless, she was worried.

She thought maybe she should telephone Easedale Police Station.

3.40 a.m.

Hunt was under the shower. Hot, needle jets were necessary in order to clear sleep, and even thought of sleep, from his mind. Murder wasn't a come-day-go-day crime out in the wilds of Calfordshire. This meant that every time that crime was committed, the constabulary pump had to be re-primed. What amounted to a fresh Murder Squad had to be created. From what he had at the scene – from the men and women who were officers of the division in which the killing had taken place – a team had to be built; a team capable of tracking down whoever was responsible and (more than that) collecting and presenting the evidence needed to convict.

It was a headache he could have done without.

This, on top of the blasted bungalow.

And yet, it had seemed so right at the time. So obvious. Rented rooms at *his* age. Furniture, carpets, curtains . . . none of which he owned. Christ, he was only a lodger on this earth. He was little more than a paying guest and, as such, tolerated by the rest of mankind.

In the fairly distant past – when Victoria had been alive and when young Edward had been at home – the house had been okay. It had seemed full; almost overflowing when Edward had asked some of his buddies round. Then Vic had died, Edward had married and, quite suddenly, he'd felt like a pea in a gasometer. Too much space. A damn sight too much space; empty space filled to bursting with memories. Then he'd moved up, from chief inspector to superintendent, moved into Calford – and decided to make the break both clean and savage. Out with the furniture, out with the books and the pictures, out with all her clothes. Out with *everything*, and find decent rooms in which he could pop his personal bibs and bobs; a place in which to sleep and little else.

Then he'd learned what loneliness really meant.

And, of course, the bungalow had been a real snip. Two bedrooms, a bathroom, a fair sized lounge and a tiny, but well equipped kitchen. *And* standing in its own little quarter-acre of ground. *And* freehold. The price had been almost giveaway and the agent had telephoned Hunt with the details within an hour of the property coming onto the market.

That had been mid-March and Hunt had moved in in late-April. Cash on the nose. Good secondhand furniture. All the bits and pieces he'd figured he needed to make life pleasant . . . and, boy, had he been wrong.

He'd been buying every day since.

He'd been *working* every day since. Work, on top of his real work as a top-of-the-bill jack. Decorating. First the lounge. Then the bedrooms, the bathroom and the kitchen. The damn doors . . . It was only when you owned property – when you decided to decorate the property yourself – that you realised how many bloody doors even the most modest of dwellings needed. Doors, and

22

windows, and skirting boards.

But it had happened. The last lick of paint had been applied. The last gloss finish had been admired. Then – almost unexpectedly – Hunt had realised that he also owned a garden.

It wasn't that he'd forgotten the infernal garden. The truth was, until now he hadn't had time to remember it. Until now it had all been sanding down, stripping off, facing up, sizing, under-coating and finishing. But the Assistant Chief Constable had seen the garden. He'd spotted it, when passing in his car, and he'd called Hunt into his office.

'Not a lot to do with me, Hunt. Just that you might not have noticed. That garden of yours. At your new place. It needs some work on it . . . don't you think?'

'It needs some work on it.' Hunt had answered in a flat emotionless voice. A voice which had left no doubt in the ACC's mind. Hunt had added, 'As you say, sir. Not a lot to do with you.'

It had been the latest in the running war between the two men, and it was both silly and non-productive. Two grown men, their chemistry and their personalities at odds, and they couldn't reach a working compromise.

The exchange had taken place two days ago and, as he slipped the soap into its dish within the shower cubicle, Hunt remembered it. He frowned at the memory and muttered, 'Oh, sod it,' then stood directly under the spray and allowed the water to clear away every last vestige of suds. Maybe he had made a mistake with the bungalow. If so, it had been made, and it couldn't be unmade.

Hangman's Lane was becoming distinctly cool. Not cold; the night frosts had not yet arrived, but for the couple of hours before dawn the temperature dropped quite noticeably. Could be it was the contrast of a scorcher of a day – a brassy sun belting its rays from a cloudless sky – and a cooling breeze that had sprung up since around midnight.

Poole remembered. The weathermen had promised

23

another hot and sticky day. Somewhere in the Atlantic a great bank of cloud was edging its way east, but whether the present high would allow its passage was anybody's guess. And if it did, it was going to be another forty-eight hours before any rain crossed the Irish Sea.

Meanwhile, it was going to be hot. Bloody hot.

That's what the clown with the weather map had said, but the clown with the weather map wasn't standing around in Hangman's Lane. He wasn't passing his time listening to the grass grow.

Poole shoved his hands into the pockets of his trousers, stamped his feet gently and, in little more than a whisper, said, 'Talk about time standing still.'

'There'll be movement enough when Hunt arrives.' Eccles sounded as if he was speaking from personal experience.

'You think . . . murder?' Poole asked the question very tentatively.

'What else?' Eccles's tone showed surprise.

'Inspector Mantell . . .' began Poole.

'Did he say not murder?'

'Well, no, but . . . he wasn't, y'know, quite sure.'

'A careful man, Inspector Mantell.'

'Aye. I suppose.'

'Doesn't like committing himself.'

'Aye, well, y'know . . . careful. Like you say.'

'Careful.' Eccles sucked his teeth noisily. 'Like an old woman wobbling around riding a bicycle. A bit of a bloody nuisance to everybody but himself.'

There was a silence. Eccles seemed to have nothing more to add, and Poole didn't feel like being too critical of an inspector in front of another of its kind.

One of the squad car officers was strolling up and down the lane. About twenty yards in one direction, then turn and walk about twenty yards back again. Going nowhere. Keeping the chill at bay. Killing time. As he passed the gate he flicked on his torch and shone it at the body. The beam quivered a little as he spoke.

'Holy cow! She's moved.'

24

'Eh?' Poole almost jumped to bring himself alongside the squad car officer.

'She's *moved*. She's not in the same position she was in last time I looked.'

'He's right.' A third torch beam joined the other two as Eccles spoke. 'She's almost on her back. She was far more on her side.'

The torch beams swung around the area of the corpse and for a moment, twin specks of deep red light looked back at them.

Poole said, 'Christ! Cats!'

'Cats be damned,' growled Eccles. 'It's a fox.'

'You mean . . .' The squad car officer seemed to choke on the question he wanted to ask.

'Fresh meat,' said Eccles flatly. 'A thing we should have remembered. *I* should have remembered.'

'What's that?'

'Way back – years ago – when I was section sergeant. Like you. One night, like tonight, cattle strayed onto a railway line. Out in the country. Like this. A passing goods train. One cow killed. Two badly injured. We had to wait for a slaughterman to arrive.' He paused to take a deep breath. 'It was fox country. I tell you, sergeant. We had to detail men to keep them off. They smell fresh, raw meat – they taste fresh, raw meat . . . well, you have your hands full.'

Poole whispered, 'Good God!'

'Stand by the body, sergeant.' Eccles jerked his head. His voice had a soft, weary quality. 'Take the motor patrolman with you. It's not a nice detail, but it's very necessary.'

3.45 a.m.

Police Constable 1009 Thomas Boyle suffered a grave and disabilitating flaw. He could never make himself look like a copper. He wore the uniform, he strolled the pavements, occasionally he reported some wrongdoer for summons, sometimes (as now) he worked Office Duty and

25

telephonically co-ordinated the various coppers of Easedale Section. It made not a scrap of difference. He neither looked the part nor acted the part.

The truth was, Boyle was a walking optical illusion.

He didn't look tall enough to be a policeman. As sure as hell, he didn't look broad enough. He looked a narrowgutted, whipcord of a guy . . . and then only if you wanted to be moderately congratulatory.

He allowed his hair to grow slightly longer than the regulations suggested, and he sported a full set of whiskers. Because of some imbalance in his bodily make-up, his hair was Persil white. It had been since his teenage years. Ergo, put a policeman's helmet on his head and the impression was of a fugitive from a Snow White pantomime.

Nor did his mannerisms kybosh that first impression. Moderation was something Tommy Boyle rarely handled. His speech was in perpetual over-drive. He waved his arms and manipulated his hands far more than was necessary. And when enthusing, there was nothing he didn't claim to know . . . until the surface was scratched, and then his self-proclaimed 'knowledge' disappeared down the nearest john.

And yet Boyle was a happy man. He was sure of himself; sure enough never to feel any embarrassment when he was made to look a clown, however many times he was made to look a clown, and however big a clown he was made to look.

Take, for example, Easedale Police Station.

Originally it had been built as Local Government Offices. There was a stone plaque near the entrance, which informed anybody interested that the first turf had been cut in 1902, and that the building had been officially opened three years later.

That did nothing to faze Boyle. It was a Grade Two listed building, therefore it had to be Victorian.

Given an ear to bend, he'd say, 'Victorian, see? You can tell by the pitch of the roof. The windows. The proportions. Betjeman knew all about proportion.'

And if the listener stared at him and said, 'Betjeman?'

'Sir John. The architect. He was potty about getting

everything just right.'

'The *architect!* He was a poet.'

'Oh, aye. He was a bit of a poet in his spare time. But the thing he was potty about was proportion. Victorian proportions. Potty. Couldn't get enough of it.'

The truth was that Police Constable Boyle had kidded himself into believing that he truly loved Easedale nick; that he was a very privileged little copper to be allowed to work from this building, with its Preservation Order attached. The less knowledgeable complained about the draughts, or griped about the lack of space. But that was only because they were bloody peasants. They didn't know, therefore they couldn't appreciate, the finer points of life . . . like having a Victorian building as a base from which to work.

The door from the foyer opened and Police Sergeant James Backhouse entered.

'On duty already?' Boyle sounded very surprised.

'Percy's scooped up this other thing.' Backhouse placed a tiny suitcase, in which was his mid-morning meal, on top of a chest-high filing cabinet. 'We can forget straightforward shift changes for a while.'

'Something happened? Something I should know about?'

'Meaning you don't know?'

'What?'

'Wardle's wife?'

'What about Wardle's wife?' Boyle sounded cross.

Backhouse waved Boyle into a chair and, as the constable's bottom touched the seat, he said, 'Wardle's wife's been murdered.'

'Oh, no!'

'Wardle found her dead, in a field somewhere.'

'Mother of God, that's bad.'

'Eccles has been out to Gauntley. At the moment he's back at Beechwood Brook organising an enquiry team for first light.'

Boyle blew out his cheeks.

Backhouse continued, 'Poole's still at the scene, that's why I'm here.'

'Nobody tells me,' muttered Boyle. 'Nobody tells me a

thing.'

'You know now.'

'Yeah, but . . .'

'From what I gather, the media people don't know yet. I think Eccles would like to keep it that way, until he decides.'

But Backhouse was wrong. 'The media', in the shape of the local rag, already knew something had happened. And all because the local postmaster couldn't sleep. He'd had a tooth extraction the previous day, and the cavity in his gums was still giving him gyp.

He'd prowled the cottage alongside the shop. He'd left the curtains open and had gazed out into the night as he'd waited for aspirins to ease the throb in his mouth. He'd seen the traffic driving through the village.

Before he'd returned to bed, he'd telephoned his brother.

'Hey, kid. Something's happened up here at Gauntley. Police cars and ambulances. I dunno what, but it has to be *something*.'

The local postmaster's name was Logan.

His younger brother's name was Fred, and Fred Logan was a very ambitious reporter on the *Beechwood Brook Chronicle*.

4.00 a.m.

Poole watched the sky give a hint of brightness from the east. The background to the silhouetted hedges seemed less dark. In another hour what was now black, dark greys and blues would gradually take on true colours; what few clouds were still around would be wispy scarves against the multi-coloured blaze of dawn.

He murmured, 'A hell of a night, if ever there was one.'

'We're so helpless,' complained the motor patrol officer. 'I feel we should be doing something.'

'What, for example?'

'There's the next-of-kin.'

28

'Wardle. He's in hospital. I thought you . . .'
'Not him. His daughter.'
'Eh?'
'He has a girl. Madge, I think. I've met her at various social do's. She and my lass get on well together. I just hope . . .'
'Oh, Christ!'
'Why? What . . .'
But Poole was already on his way, hurrying across the grass and to the gate leading onto the lane.

4.10 a.m.

To have a name like Adam Suchet, and also to be in the police force was, perhaps, bad enough. To have blond hair and to wear it slightly longer than might be thought appropriate, was pushing things.

Nevertheless, Suchet had reached the rank of inspector, and had recently moved into the post of Scene of Crime Officer. It meant that he attended every serious crime; it meant that (with the blessing of a senior ranker who happened to be in charge of the enquiry) he instigated certain standard police procedures; it meant that he worked in close collaboration with Lessford Forensic Science Laboratory in the job of searching for and finding hairs, fibres, glass chipping, paint flakes, blood splashes and general minute debris with which the various boffins might play and (sometimes) assist in the conviction of a criminal.

The job of Scene of Crime Officer demanded a certain type of brain. A fiddling brain. A brain which dwelt upon seemingly unimportant and insignificant trifles. A brain capable of absolute concentration.

The telephone bell had awakened Suchet from his sleep. He'd immediately recognised Hunt's voice.

'. . . and I'm at Force Headquarters. I'll be leaving for Easedale within fifteen minutes. I want you to be with me.'

'Yes, sir.' Suchet swung his feet from the bed and onto

the lino. 'If you could call for me . . .'

'*Call* for you.'

'It's on your way, sir. It would save . . .'

'This isn't a cab service, Suchet. Move your arse out of those silk pyjamas or whatever you wear, and *be* here. You savvy that?'

'Yes, bwana. To hear is to obey, oh Great One.' Suchet's voice was soft. His tone was of controlled contempt. 'The noble master opens his cake-hole. His slave trembles in terrified apprehension.'

The chances were that Hunt heard at least the opening sentences of the sardonic murmurings. Whether he replied, or not, Suchet didn't know. As he finished speaking, he lowered the handset and placed it gently – almost daintily – back on its rest.

Police Constable 1009 Boyle was one of those individuals who hate silence. The mouth was made to be used. Use it. Talk. Forget all the crap about silence being golden. Talk . . . about *anything*.

Police Sergeant Backhouse, on the other hand, had just been dragged from a deep and refreshing sleep. Without being actually peeved – without wishing to find serious fault with a system that hauled him out on duty at ungodly hours – he was in no mood for idle chatter.

From Boyle's point of view, therefore, it was a little like rowing up-stream against a particularly strong current. Nevertheless, he tried.

'Nice day,' he tendered. Then as an after-thought added, 'It's going to be hot again tomorrow.'

'Tomorrow?'

'When the sun gets up.'

'It's going to be hot again,' agreed Backhouse.

In the distance, and from Easedale Sidings, came the clank and hiss of some sort of shunting operation.

'A bit too hot,' tried Boyle. 'I mean – y'know – it can be *too* hot.'

'Can it?'

'Yes. Well, er, no . . . not if you like it hot. I mean, if you

30

like heat, it can never be too hot. Can it?'

'I don't mind.' Backhouse seemed to deliberately throw the conversational ball back at Boyle. With complete non-interest, he added, 'Do you?'

'Eh?'

'Mind?'

'Mind what?'

'The heat?'

'Yes. Well, no . . . I don't mind the heat.'

'Good.'

'Eh? Oh, er, yes.' Boyle moved his lips together in an attempt to remove the dryness. It made his beard waggle and made him look slightly ridiculous. He blurted out, 'Holidays. Are you, I mean, are you . . . are you taking holiday leave soon?'

'No. Why?'

'I just, y'know, wondered. A lot of the lads are.' Boyle opened and closed his mouth a couple of times – much like a fish taking ant eggs – then croaked, 'Sergeant, do you, I mean would you . . . do you mind telling me, more or less, what's going on?'

'I thought I'd told you.'

'Yes, but . . . Tabs Wardle. I mean – y'know – is it, *murder?*'

'What else?'

'No. I suppose. But – y'know – what do we do?'

'Do?'

'You. Me. What do we *do?* I've only read about it. In books. Thrillers. Agatha Christie things. I haven't much of an idea what we are supposed to—'

'We,' said Backhouse gruffly, 'are "supposed" to do exactly what we're told. No fancy Sherlock Holmes stuff. Nothing likely to startle the horses. We just stand around like so many prats. Try to look intelligent. Tell nobody a bloody thing . . . and hope nobody tumbles.'

'Tumbles?'

'That we haven't a clue, lad. That you and me – that everybody under the rank of inspector – is only here to brew the tea and fetch the fags.'

31

'Oh!'

From the alcove to one side of the room the telephone bell rang.

Boyle answered the call and, when he returned to the main office, he looked very worried.

'Trouble?' asked Backhouse.

'Nobody's told Madge yet,' said Boyle.

'Madge?'

'Madge. Wardle's daughter. Her mother's been murdered. Her father's flat out in some hospital ward. And nobody's got round to letting *her* know a thing.'

'Cock-ups,' said Backhouse flatly.

'Eh?'

'Cock-ups. Snarl-ups. The bigger the crime, the bigger the balls-ups. You asked me what coppers like us can do. I'll tell you. We can duck. And why? Because the bollocks will be flying in our direction twenty-four hours a day.' He blew out his cheeks, then added, 'Get Phillips. Tell her to be here as soon as she can. We've one of those jobs to do . . . one of those jobs they don't mention before you join.'

4.30 a.m.

Way back, some years after Hitler's war, Fred Logan — then still a schoolboy — had seen a re-run of the film *His Girl Friday*. The film, from the Ben Hecht re-write of the Charles Leaderer play, *The Front Page*, had been, and still was, one of those milestones in cinema history; the pace had been right, the casting had been perfect and Howard Hawks' directing had been as near magical as to make no difference. Young Logan had seen the film three times in one week. From that moment, his career had been nailed to any door anybody cared to open.

He was going to be a newspaperman.

And he was, indeed, a newspaperman. From leaving school he'd aimed his nose in that one direction and, by the age of eighteen, he was attending local weddings, funerals and vicarage tea-parties and being careful not to mis-spell any of the names.

Not quite Cary Grant stuff, but what the hell?

The hell was that, try as he may, Logan moved only slowly and painfully from that lower rung of reporting. He'd tried, but he hadn't the knack. He was too long-winded. Too 'purple'. Given the opportunity he'd choose a fifteen-cylinder word which half the readers hadn't even heard of before, instead of a simple Anglo-Saxon remark which hit them straight between the eyes.

As the editor had said, not once, but many times, 'Fred, in this game you're backing honest-to-goodness bread. Leave the soufflés to those who fancy *cordon bleu* fussiness.'

And now, thanks to a brother with toothache, he was on the way to a scoop. He'd finish up as a stringer for one of the nationals. He'd have his own by-line . . . that or nobody would get the full story.

Meanwhile . . .

He vaulted a gate and, keeping in the shadow of the hedges, made his way towards where, across the fields, the reflection of lights and the shadows of movement pin-pointed the place where the activity was taking place.

4.45 a.m.

Dilly Phillips liked her job. Even at this hour – even with a detail like this – she still liked her job.

'Somebody had to do it,' she said. 'We'll do it kindly.'

'Kindly?' Backhouse's expression was deliberately hard. He squinted into the gloom of a not-yet-opened day and, as much as possible, concentrated upon driving the car. 'You think there's an easy option on a job like this?'

'I think there are different ways of doing it.'

'Hard and soft?' mocked Backhouse, but the mockery was a put-on and Policewoman Phillips knew Backhouse well enough to recognise the put-on.

'Gently and not so gently. As coppers or as friends.'

'We're coppers, miss,' said Backhouse gruffly. 'At this moment – for the next few hours – we're strictly coppers.'

She was silent for a few moments, as if digesting the obliquely given advice, then she said, 'That won't make it easier for Madge.'

'No. Maybe not.'

'She'll want *friends*.'

'There'll be others. Somebody.'

'Hopefully.' Dilly Phillips sighed, then continued, 'Do we find one first?'

'What?'

'One of those "friends" . . . assuming you're right. Assuming she has any.'

'I can't see what you're getting at.'

'Sergeant, you can see.' Dilly Phillips sounded cross. 'You're just pretending not to see. Contact this "friend", break the news to her, then let her do the dirty work.'

'I made no such . . .'

'We aren't "friends", we're coppers,' snapped Phillips. 'That's the lead-in. That's the next step. It's been done before, sergeant. If it's done this time we'll both feel the shame.'

Backhouse's jaw muscles tightened a little. He stared ahead, into the gloom of a day not yet quite dawned; into headlight beams which couldn't quite clear away the grey dimness of the hour.

The bloody woman was right. But she'd no business being right. This miserable affair had started at about midnight – that's what he, Backhouse, had been told – and the next-of-kin hadn't yet been notified. Poole was being his usual prattish self. So was Mantell. It had been their job – so obviously *their* job – but, as usual, people had conveniently 'forgotten' to do the more distasteful jobs. Memories, you see. They slip cogs when things get too hairy.

He muttered, 'Shame? It's them that should feel shame.'

'Who?' Being unaware of Backhouse's thought process, Phillips couldn't latch onto the sergeant's remark. 'Who should be ashamed?'

'The idle buggers who haven't done their jobs.'

'Who?'

'Those who found the body. About midnight. That's

when they knew who it was. Four hours back – at least four hours – and they haven't yet notified the next-of-kin.'

'I'm not looking forward to it either,' she said, gently. She was wise enough to know what was behind his complaining. 'But somebody has to do it. Let's try to make Madge glad that it was us.'

Henry Boothroyd lay in the bed of his tied cottage and stared into the near-darkness of pre-dawn. The prickling behind his eyes made him feel even more sorry for himself, and soon the tears would well from his eyes and roll down his cheeks.

That silly magistrate, yesterday. He was there to decide – to punish – not to pass moral judgement. He was too bloody old, anyway. For a fact, there wouldn't be much lead left in his pencil.

From the next bedroom he could hear the soft snore of his mother's slumber. She'd be on her back. She'd have her mouth open. That hint of bubbling from the back of her throat . . . it was always there.

The stupid, wicked old bitch.

It was all her fault, of course. All this jumping out in front of women, and opening his raincoat. All *her* fault. He could remember. When he was a kid. Before he even started school. *And* after. She couldn't keep her disgusting fingers off him. The arse, the crotch, the balls . . . everywhere. She gloried in working him up, until he had a bar on. Then she'd go the whole hog, and soften the bar.

Christ! He hadn't known. At first he'd been too young to know. Then – later – it had been too late. Too late for anything. Only this. Only flashing himself in front of strange women. Only being nicked for it. Only being bawled out by a magistrate who didn't know the half of it. Only having ignorant coppers, like Wardle, label him as a pervert. As a frustrated rapist.

As if he would.

As if he *could*.

The tears spilled over and, in the next room, his mother stopped snoring.

*

Logan crept forward across the dew-wet grass. In truth, he felt something of a prat, but to listen without being seen – to hear something not meant for ears other than police ears – was well worth looking a prat for.

He kept his eyes fixed on the other side of the hedge. On where two policemen – one helmeted and the other wearing a peaked cap – were standing chatting to each other. Beyond them – beyond the field in which they stood and beyond another hedge – more coppers were milling around. Some in uniform. One man in plain clothes . . . but he had to be a copper, if only because those in uniform treated him with unusual, fawning respect.

Logan could, by this time, catch words spoken by the two officers nearest to him.

'So, I said to him. I said, "You won't get much bloody mileage out of that clapped-out heap".'

'But he still bought it?'

'Oh, aye. They won't be told.'

'That's a fact.'

'Everbody's an expert. Everybody knows all about motor cars.'

'And what d'you think he'd done, then? To make it run smoother?'

'Sawdust.'

'Eh?'

'Sawdust, in the gear box. That's all it needed. A handful of sawdust in the gearbox. Plenty of oil—'

The motor patrol officer stopped in mid-sentence as Logan planted the palm of one hand into a fresh and juicy cow pat and, in so doing, let out a quick snort of disgust.

A torch beam wavered from the other side of the hedge. It groped around for a moment, then landed full on Logan's upturned face.

Police Sergeant Poole held the torch steady, and said, 'My word, and what breed of crawling little insect have we here?'

36

5.00 a.m.

Suchet drove. Hunt relaxed in the front passenger seat. It was Hunt's car, a not-too-ancient Rover, but that didn't matter. Suchet was a better driver than Hunt, and Hunt knew it. It also gave Hunt the mental freedom to out-smart-talk Suchet . . . or so he thought. Equally, it gave Suchet a half-excuse to make-believe he didn't quite catch what Hunt said . . . if such a ploy was necessary.

'Scene of Crime Officer,' murmured Hunt derisively. 'Now, what the hell does that mean, I wonder?'

'It's a job,' said Suchet flatly.

'Jobs for the boys,' sneered Hunt. 'At least, a job for one of the boys.'

The outskirts of the county town, Calford, were by this time a couple of miles behind. At that hour, the road was almost denuded of traffic. The needle of the speedometer hovered between sixty-five and seventy.

'I have eyes,' said Suchet teasingly. He added, 'In time a white stick – perhaps a guide dog – will be standard issue to all CID personnel.'

'Including me?' The question had warning signs attached.

'I feel sorry for you, Chief Superintendent.' Despite the words, the tone said 'the hell I do'. Suchet continued, 'The idea that people like the standard plain clothes man being in charge of anything more involved than Hunt the Thimble fills me with trepidation.'

'Is that a fact?'

'In time, my own Lords and Masters will be . . .'

'Your "Lords and Masters"?'

'The forensic scientists.'

'The Test Tube Babies?'

'Mock them not, Chief Superintendent Hunt. They are fast approaching the point where they'll be able to point you to the man who committed any crime they attend.'

'Meaning any crime *you* attend?'

'I know what to look for. I even know how to look.'

'All right . . . this crime. The one we're going to.' Hunt

37

relaxed in his seat and, like a mischievous cat, played games with a mouse which wasn't quite as helpless as he might have wished it to be. He said, 'A woman. Not young, closing up to fifty at a guess. A village copper's wife. She's been murdered.' He paused, then ended, 'First reactions?'

'Scientists deal in facts, Chief Superintendent. Not reaction.'

'You're a scientist?' murmured Hunt mockingly.

'I work for scientists.'

'I don't.' Hunt closed his eyes. The impression was that he was talking quietly to himself. Testing theories, perhaps. Or, perhaps, putting tiny bricks of necessary logic into place. He said, 'Let's say sex, as a motive. As a reason for killing her. That means extra-marital humping. If her husband found out? Ah, but he's a copper. He knows what he's up against.'

'Up against?' This time it was Suchet who asked a question heavy with sarcasm.

'All those scientists.' Hunt opened his eyes long enough to glance sideways. 'All that high-powered brainwork. All those Scene of Crime Officers.'

'It needn't be sex.'

'As sure as hell it's not money . . . not on a village bobby's pay.'

'They're not badly paid these days.'

'We're talking about murder, Suchet. We're talking about spending the rest of your life behind granite. We're talking about going to prison where, whatever else you've done, being a copper is the worst crime of all.' He smiled a twisted smile. 'Have you ever talked to coppers who've slipped, and spent time in prison?'

'No. I can't say—'

'*I* have. That's one section of the community that will go straight. All the old lags inside enjoy the game of "getting even". Pissing in the tea before handing you a mug is one of the lesser aggravations.'

'That's not civilised.'

'Of course it isn't. Nor is killing a fellow human being.'

'That's why—'

38

'That's why,' interrupted Hunt, 'the world needs equally uncivilised bastards . . . like me. We catch 'em. We squeeze the truth out of 'em. You – and your "Lords and Masters" – tidy things up, put all the punctuation marks in the right place . . . pin the animals to the nearest door with tiny thumb-tacks of "scientific evidence".'

Madge Wardle guessed the truth before either Police-woman Phillips or Sergeant Backhouse said one word likely to indicate their reason for being there. She guessed, because she was a policeman's daughter. Because of the time. Because neither her father nor her mother had returned home. Perhaps, most of all, she guessed the truth because, for some hours, her own imagination had been at work, all the permutations of various possibilities had been thought about and discarded so that only the stark truth remained.

As they left the hall of the police house and walked into the living room, Phillips said, 'Sit down, Madge,' and those words were a mere verification.

As she lowered herself into an armchair, Madge Wardle breathed, 'He's dead, isn't he?'

'Come on, luv. Just relax. Y'know . . . relax.'

Backhouse said, 'It's not your dad, Madge. It's your mother.'

'Mother?'

'Sorry.' And, indeed, Backhouse was genuinely sorry. He truly hated being the bearer of bad news.

'Has – has . . .' Madge Wardle's eyes took on a wild look.

'Easy, luv,' cooed Phillips.

Madge's hands gripped the arms of the chair and she choked, 'Oh Lord! Has he killed her!'

'She's – er – she's been killed,' Backhouse figured it better to push ahead and get the thing said. 'I'm afraid she's dead, pet.'

'He's killed her?'

'Who?'

'Dad. That's why he's not . . .'

'No, no.' Backhouse shook his head. 'He's – er – he's

helping, that's all.'

'I know. "Helping with enquiries". I know what that means.'

'Look, luv. Will you please—'

'And will you please stop fussing!' The words were snapped into Policewoman Phillips' face. The younger woman then turned to Backhouse and said, 'Mother's dead?'

'I'm sorry . . . . yes.'

'Killed?'

'Yes.' Backhouse nodded.

'Murdered?'

'We – er – we think so.'

'By Dad?'

'We don't know.' Backhouse tried, desperately, to get through to this tough young lady. It was all wrong. By all the rules of the game, she should be flooding the place with tears. Hysterical, maybe. Even having an attack of the vapours. Instead, she seemed the least upset of the three . . . which, admittedly, wasn't saying much. He continued, 'I'm not pulling punches, Madge. Your mother's been shot. Your dad's in hospital recovering from the shock.'

'You'd tell me?' Backhouse thought he heard the hint of a tremble in her voice, as she insisted, 'You *would* tell me?'

'Your mother's dead,' said Backhouse softly. 'I haven't seen her, but I understand she's been shot.'

'Where?'

'I don't know. As I say, I haven't seen—'

'No, I mean *where*? Whereabouts? In Gauntley? Somewhere else?'

'Oh. In Gauntley. Hangman's Lane . . . so I'm told.'

'And Dad isn't in custody?'

'He's in hospital. He found her. The shock. I mean, you can't really expect much else. It must have been – have been . . .' Backhouse's voice trailed off to silence.

The girl was staring up at him and, although her expression remained fixed and without any sign of emotion, her eyes filled and the tears spilled over. It was something Backhouse had never witnessed before.

She didn't seem to realise that she was crying.

Detective Sergeant Moody did the grilling, with Detective Inspector Eccles being an interested witness. Fred Logan was being grilled, was not enjoying the experience and was quite sure Cary Grant would never have tolerated the going over to which he was being subjected.

'A newshound?'

Moody asked the question as if he had grave doubts; as if he figured that Logan had made a wild guess in a vain attempt to give some sort of cockeyed explanation for his antics.

'I'm from the Press,' spluttered Logan.

'Gutter?'

'Eh?'

'It would go some way towards explaining things.'

'Something's happened here.'

'Of course. That or it's a policeman's convention . . . and it's not that.'

'That's why.' Logan tried to bluff it out.

'Why what?'

'Why I'm here. Why I'm making enquiries.'

'Making *enquiries!* You snivelling little toe-rag. You insignificant little crawler. You were on your hands and knees, creeping around, trying to hear things you shouldn't.'

'I don't see why—'

'Who told you?' snapped Moody.

'Eh?'

'About this lot. Who told you? Who told you to come creeping around fishing for whatever you could get?'

'I have my informants.' Logan tried haughtiness for size.

'I guessed that much. Not for one moment did I think you had crystal balls.'

'I'm not allowed to divulge the people who—'

'You'll "divulge",' said Moody grimly. He turned to Eccles and asked, 'One of the squad cars to take him to Beechwood Brook nick?'

'Of course,' nodded Eccles.

'He can sit in a cell until we've time to ask him a few questions.'

'Look!' Panic began to set in. Logan's eyes flicked between the two officers as he spoke. 'I'll help. Of course I will. Anything you want to know—'

'It doesn't matter.' Moody's tone dropped to a low, bored level. 'You'll help . . . of course you will. You're down the pot, Logan. And I have the handle of the chain ready in my hand.' Moody beckoned to a nearby squad man and, when that officer came to within easy hearing distance, continued, 'Frederick Logan. He'll give you his home address when you ask. Meanwhile, he's nicked. Suspected Murder. Slap him in a Beechwood Brook cell. Incommunicado until further notice. *Strictly* incommunicado. No questions. No smart-arse lawyer until I'm there to make it a three-sided contest. Feed him, water him, forget him. Understood?'

'Understood, sir.'

The squad man moved in and touched Logan's arm.

Logan jumped away, and rapped, 'If you think I'm going to let you—'

'Don't make trouble,' snapped the motor patrol officer and made a firmer grab at the arm.

There was a slight struggle. The squad man took one side. Eccles took the other. Logan twisted and turned a little, but the handcuffs stopped all further stupidity.

When the reporter was safely in the squad car, and the car was pulling away down Hangman's Lane, Eccles said, 'He is, of course, from the local daily. I've seen him around.'

'Me, too,' grunted Moody. 'He's a bloody nuisance.'

'He might,' observed Eccles, 'kick up a fuss.'

'No doubt he will.'

'Unlawful arrest . . . that sort of thing.'

'Crawling around on his hands and knees at the scene of a murder. If he gets away with—'

'This might help.' Eccles held out a cheap but flash ballpoint pen. 'It, er, "fell from his pocket", during that slight scuffle.'

'Oh!' Moody took the proffered ballpoint.

Very airily, Eccles added, 'I rather suspect it "fell from his

42

pocket" near the body. At the scene of the crime. Which is where *you* found it. For all we know, he might have been creeping back to retrieve it . . . having shot the woman.'

A grin touched Moody's lips, as he said, 'That little scenario should loosen his bowels.'

The dope was starting to wear off. Wardle still couldn't concentrate, but he knew enough to realise he wasn't in his own bed. Not in his own bed, but in bed. A strange bed and a strange room, with a strange young woman hovering around alongside this strange bed.

He muttered, 'What is it?'

'You're all right, Mr Wardle. Just relax and go back to sleep.'

The strange woman stood alongside him. Alongside his shoulder. She lifted his left hand by the wrist and held it. With her free hand she lifted a tiny fob watch from her breast pocket and consulted it.

He muttered, 'You're not Tabs.'

'Just relax Mr Wardle. You're quite safe.'

'Where's Tabs?'

'Go back to sleep, Mr Wardle.'

'Look, I want to—'

'Just relax. Don't worry about anything. Don't even think about anything.'

'Why? You can't just . . .'

But in the same hazy, befuddled way he realised that he was alone.

Alone. Really alone. Something terrifying – but something not quite understood – tugged at his brain and insisted that, for reasons beyond his ken, he was more alone than he'd ever been in his life. The realisation widened his eyes and made him make an effort to hoist himself up on this elbows.

He couldn't make it.

He fell back onto the pillows, closed his eyes and once more he slept.

6.00 a.m.

Such an important hour. In the police world it heralded the start of a new day. Six o'clock. Not midnight. Midnight was merely a point two hours into a night shift which, in turn, was a section of yesterday's round of duties. Midnight belonged to another day. To a day now past. But six o'clock meant a new and untouched gathering of eight-hour sessions. No shift overlapped that six o'clock in the morning spot. Everything stopped on or before that time. Everything was, indeed, new and unwrapped.

Not that things looked new and unwrapped at Easedale Police Station, but that wasn't the fault of the time of day, nor yet of the day itself. From the day it had been built Easedale nick had looked old, if not actually ancient. Easedale was only a small community, but despite this it was a rich and busy one. It 'made' things – things like bricks, things like steel castings, things like dyestuffs – and the more it made the thicker the dirt which spread itself upon every external surface of the town.

The station was the hub of Easedale Police Section. Its nick was the 'base' for the fifteen coppers whose job it was to squash the enthusiasm of would-be criminals within its population. Yet although the bulk of Easedale Section was made up of rural areas – of trees and forests, of farms and hamlets, of open sky and good clean air – the Town Beats were as urban as any beat in Leeds, Bradford or Manchester. Its stone lintels and sills were thick with grime. The brickwork between was pock-marked with an accumulation of soot. The windows had grey grubbiness fixed hard to their surface. Throughout the years the whole outside of the structure had been sand-blasted with tiny particles of dirt . . . and it showed and would show forever.

Nothing ever looked new at Easedale Police Station.

There was a room at the rear of the building. It was on the ground floor and, once upon a time, it had been provisionally earmarked as a 'Billiard Room'. Nothing had happened. The Police Authority had turned a deaf ear to

44

the first tentative suggestions that enough cash for a billiard table for one of the section stations be gently eased in the appropriate direction.

The room had had other uses since. Identification parades had been mounted within its walls. Lectures given to the local Special Constables occupied the room periodically. At General Elections and Local Elections the collapsible voting booths were stored there, handy for collection on the evening before the big day. It was that sort of a room. Large, without being massive. Not particularly uncomfortable, but in winter not particularly warm.

At the moment – at six of the clock, ante meridian, this beautiful Wednesday – the room was being used as a Briefing Room. If necessary it would also be used as a Murder Room, but that would be jumping the gun slightly.

Hunt lorded it over the assembly which consisted of fifteen other officers, some sitting on chairs but most of them standing around, listening. Suchet had gone on ahead to check the scene of the crime. But Mantell was there, as were two uniformed sergeants. The PBI consisted of four detective constables, two beat coppers, two policewomen and two motor patrol officers. Two hurriedly summoned Special Constabulary men made up the assorted bunch. It wasn't much for a manhunt, but Mantell had done his best. Hunt sniffed slight disdain at the motley collection, but this was real-life. This wasn't some TV cops-and-robbers saga, where extra officers could be dragged in from Central Casting.

Hunt stood straddle-legged in front of an easel upon which rested a scratched and pitted blackboard. Because of what he was – because of his elephantine personality – he used words and phrases which, from a less assured man, might have sounded marginally silly. From Hunt they sounded quite normal.

'There's a killer out there, ladies and gentlemen. No ordinary killer. He's murdered the wife of a colleague. That, alone, makes this enquiry something special.

45

'Forget the Book of Words. Forget the garbage you might have been told on various Detective courses, Home Office courses and the like. The goons who spout at those establishments couldn't detect their way from one end of a drainpipe to the other . . . they wouldn't be hidden away talking about it, were it otherwise. They'd be out here doing it. Polishing up the Crime Statistics.

'You'll work in pairs. Each pair will have a clipboard and foolscap. Everything is timed and logged. *Everything*. If you have to knock off for a quick pee, fine . . . but log it.

'Timing. Documentation. That's the thing. Tabitha Wardle is dead. She isn't going anywhere. There's no great hurry. I want no smooth-talking lawyer hooking a pseudo-defence onto some sloppy interviewing. The hell with speed. I want accuracy, and I want questions asked, answered and recorded.

'Every forty-five minutes – thereabouts – take time off and what you've recorded on your foolscap and clipboards, enter into your notebooks. *Everything*. When – if – you come under cross-examination, I want you to be able to refer to your notebook entries and give a straight, unvarnished answer. No fannying. No lying. No "ifs", no "buts" . . . if anybody's going to look a prize prat, I want it to be the bewigged clown asking the questions.'

Hunt paused. He looked around the room. In turn, his eyes rested on each man and woman present. For a second or so he stared into each face.

He said, 'All I do is interview suspects. I try to tie 'em up in a cat's cradle of lies. If I succeed, it's because you people have collected enough bits and pieces of truth to allow me to succeed. For the moment, that's what you're doing. For the moment, everybody you talk to – *everybody* – could be the killer.'

Eccles and Suchet were quietly setting the stage for the star performer. Such was the impression . . . and it wasn't far from the truth. Both men had climbed to the rank of inspector. Nor was there much difference between a detective inspector and an inspector which was the rank of a Scene of Crime Officer. Indeed, the SCO was included in the authorised strength of the constabulary CID. All this, but they were quaking mildly at the anticipation of Hunt's arrival at the scene.

'He'll find fault,' said Suchet. 'He always does.'

'It's what he's paid for,' observed Eccles, with some philosophy.

Already plastic tape removed Hangman's Lane from the rest of the world. The tape was white, with scarlet lettering reading: *Police. Scene of Crime. No Unauthorised Person Allowed Beyond This Point* repeated monotonously along its yard upon yard of length.

'It goes with the rank,' observed Suchet sadly.

'What?'

'Pomposity.'

'Oh!' Eccles smiled. 'Y'mean Hunt.'

Moody and a couple of motor patrol officers were handling the tape. It was draped across the gate leading to the field. It marked a two-yard-wide path, across the grass and to the body. It looked quite festive. Nobody figured it was defeating its own objective; that by blazoning the presence of the police and the commission of a crime, it was attracting attention to the very spot the coppers required to be kept quiet and unobtrusive for as long as possible.

'House-to-house,' said Suchet off-handedly.

'Not many houses round here.'

'That's what I mean.'

'Less than a thousand,' mused Eccles. 'Much less than a thousand people, and that includes kids. Then there's the outlying farms.'

'One day should get the basic questions asked. That's what I mean.'

'Less.' Eccles sounded confident. 'It's rural, remember. Very rural. If it's somebody local, most of 'em will know.'

'Know?'

'Guess.' Eccles corrected himself. 'What they *will* know is the motive. Who likes who. Who hates who. Who's done who a bad turn. That sort of thing.'

Detective Sergeant Moody joined them and said, 'That's about it. Ready for the boffins and the experts to get cracking.'

'A good job?' asked Suchet mischievously.

'I reckon.'

'Hunt will disillusion you, Sergeant.'

'I can't see what the hell else he can . . .'

'You know this neck of the woods, Sergeant.' Eccles seemed to remember something. 'I mean – y'know – *know* it.'

'Well enough,' said Moody gruffly.

'A girl, wasn't it?'

'I was keen.' Moody compressed his lips. 'She broke off things. The engagement, I suppose. Unofficial, but—'

'What I mean,' interrupted Eccles, 'is that you know the place. The people. Maybe even who might have it in for Wardle.'

'Wardle?'

'His wife. Y'know . . . getting at him, through his missus.'

'I dunno?' Moody frowned. 'There's – er – Cooley. Would he do a trick like that?'

'Would he?' Eccles threw the question back.

'Possible,' mused Moody. 'He's a nasty enough bastard.'

'Who's Cooley?' asked Suchet.

'Samuel Cooley.' Eccles answered the question. 'He runs a battery-hen place on the outskirts of Gauntley.'

Moody said, 'It doesn't matter whether it pays or not. His real job is breaking.'

'Shops. Offices.' Eccles picked up the story, like a runner making a smooth change in a relay. 'Not houses. We don't think houses. He's done a couple of major post-office jobs.'

'Caught?' asked Suchet.

'Once, ten years back. Nearly a couple of times since.' Eccles pulled a face. 'The bloody Jury system.'

'Yeah, well.'

'That so-called "Reasonable Doubt". It gets 'em off. Even when we know they're as guilty as sin.'

'They're entitled to it, Sergeant.' Suchet sounded very dogmatic. 'It's one of the things that makes for civilisation.'

'And guns,' chimed in Eccles.

'Eh?'

'Guns. He belongs to a shooting club. He's keen on bang-bangs. A pound to a pinch of snuff, he goes armed when he does a job.'

'You know that?'

'Not without "Reasonable Doubt",' mocked Moody.

Eccles said, 'We'll know for sure, when he blows some poor sod away.'

Policewoman Phillips tried hard to show the understanding and compassion which she knew was required of her. Dammit, this kid had just lost her mother. Her father was flat out at the Mark Cullpepper Hospital. She was having emotional spots knocked off her, therefore she deserved sympathy *and* understanding *and* compassion.

Except, of course, Madge Wardle refused to do the things the textbook said she should be doing.

Tears?

Sure, tears. Some tears. But just a trickle. No flood. This sixteen-year-old lady seemed to have complete control of the waterworks. Equally, she had control of her voice. No catching of the breath. No facial expression showing massive grief. She had control of *everything*.

She said, 'It had to happen.'

'What?' Phillips was intrigued.

'Tabs. She couldn't help herself. But that didn't make any difference. It had to happen, one day.'

'What had to happen?'

'A killing. If not a killing, a terrible hiding. Then another hiding. Then another. Maybe, in the long run, the killing was the kinder way. If she didn't suffer.'

'I – er – I don't think she suffered,' gulped Phillips.

'I'm glad.' Madge Wardle linked her fingers between her knees. She stared at them in total concentration for a moment, before she spoke. 'I've often wondered . . .' she began.

'What?'

'With Alex being a copper. Only a village copper, but a copper.'

49

'What?' repeated Phillips.

'This business of murder. As I see it, everybody's capable of killing.'

'Eh?' Phillips looked a little shocked.

'Of course they are. Something. Somebody. There's always *something, somebody, some* reason . . . you'd kill in the final analysis. Everybody would. And it's called "murder".'

'I – er – I wouldn't go along with that. I mean—'

'You would,' insisted the younger woman. 'Everybody would.'

'No. That's a terrible thing to say. That's—'

'Why terrible? What's wrong with it?'

'For heaven's sake. You can't—'

'*You* can't. Or, at least, you can't admit to it. But that's because you're a policewoman. That's why. Alex couldn't either.'

'Alex?'

'He wouldn't admit it either.'

'Alex? You mean . . .'

'My father. Alex. Didn't you know him as "Alex"?'

'Well, no. Y'know, I knew it was "Alex". I knew that was his first name. But I always called him Constable Wardle.'

'Yeah. You would.' Madge Wardle smiled a very knowing smile. 'That was him. Stand-offish. But that was because he was scared.'

'Scared?'

'Scared shitless.'

'Look, I wouldn't say he was—'

'Not *that* way. Not that sort of "scared". I mean about Tabs. About mother. Somebody might find out.'

'Look, I don't think we should—'

'People.' Madge Wardle's voice moved into a soft, sleepy drone. 'You can *tell*, don't you think? What they are. What's going to happen to them. The ones who'll be very lucky if somebody doesn't lose control and kill them. They ask for it.' She paused, then added, 'Tabs did. She *begged* for it. The wonder is she wasn't murdered long since.'

Calfordshire Air Waves was one of those local radio stations boasting an on-the-spot link with every corner of the area covered by its pop-orientated broadcasts. It sent out news, every hour, on the hour, and was not averse to breaking in on its scheduled programmes in order to pip all other local, regional and national networks with some red-hot flash of Calfordshire jiggery-pokery.

Like all media organisations, Calfordshire Air Waves had its network of listening posts. People in a position to see and hear whatever might make news, and also ready to pass the word to the Lessford studios and offices, from whence this hot-shot news service originated. And one of those listening posts was the Mark Cullpepper Hospital.

At the public counter of Easedale Police Station a tip-off from the hospital was causing some embarrassment to Police Constable Boyle.

The man with the expensive tape recorder said, 'You *must* know.'

'Oh, no.' Boyle flapped his arms a little, looked wild-eyed and gabbled, 'I don't, it's not my business to know those things. I'm in the office. Anyway, it's time I was off duty.'

The name of the man with the tape recorder was Francis – William Francis – and as he flicked a lighter and held the flame to a cigarette already in his mouth, he looked quite bored.

He said, 'I have it on the best authority.'

'I don't care. I'm sorry, but—'

'A uniformed constable – name of Wardle – admitted just after midnight. All I want to know is, why?'

'I keep telling you—'

'From this section. From Gauntley . . . so I'm told.'

'Look, I keep saying. I haven't been out of this office since ten o'clock last night. It's where I've *been*. Ever since I came on duty.'

Francis took a long draw on the cigarette. He dragged the smoke deep into his lungs, then let it out gently, via nostrils and mouth, until it formed a haze around the upper half of his face.

He murmured, 'Boy, are you scared.'

'It's not that. It's—'

51

'What is it, Constable Doyle?'

'Boyle. P.C. *Boyle* . . . with a B.'

'Boyle.' Francis nodded slowly. 'I must get the name right. Boyle.'

'Look. You mustn't—'

'Police Constable Boyle,' repeated Francis, softly and slowly. 'A man who professes an ignorance which, if true, makes him a disgrace to his uniform. A man who draws a salary well beyond his pathetic earning power. If untrue, it makes him a bare-faced liar. A man not fit to be a police constable.'

'You – you can't say that.'

'Can't I?' The lips bowed into a slow, knowing smile. 'Just you keep tuned to Calfordshire Air Waves. You'll find how very wrong you are.'

'I – I can't tell you. Good heavens, you know that.'

'Can't? Won't?' teased Francis.

'I'm not allowed to. I'd be for the high jump.'

'His name,' suggested Francis, pleasantly. 'Wardle. He arrived at Cullpepper in an ambulance. Can you at least verify *that*?'

'Yes. That's – y'know . . .' Boyle continued to flap his arms and wave his whiskers in the air a little.

'Right?' suggested Francis. 'Correct?'

Boyle nodded.

'Why did he need a hospital?'

'Eh?'

'An ambulance?'

'He was, he was . . .' Boyle dried up.

'Hurt?' suggested Francis.

'There was . . .' Boyle swallowed, then gabbled, 'A shooting.'

'A shooting?' The eyebrows and the voice went up as Francis asked the rhetorical question.

'Look. That's all I can tell you. Honest. I don't *know* anything else. Out in the back, there.' Boyle indicated with the stab of a thumb. 'Hunt. More weight than we've had here for years. There's a briefing going on. They don't tell *me* anything. If they – y'know – if they thought I was

52

telling you things, they'd go spare. So, *please*. Ask somebody else. Ask somebody who knows. I've told you all I know.'

'A briefing?' Francis took a final deep draw on the cigarette. He left it between his lips as he hefted the tape recorder from the counter with his left hand, then added, 'Something big? Something that needs a briefing . . . and by Hunt. I'll hit the horizon, Constable Boyle. Thanks for your help. It's appreciated.'

7.15 a.m.

Easedale was stretching itself after a good night's sleep. There was a gradual awakening; a busy stopping and starting of milk-delivery vans; a silent streaming out of bicycles ridden by postmen as they left the main sorting office with their sacks on the front carriers of their machines. Newspapers were being delivered to news-agents, then sorted, folded, crammed into satchels before being shouldered by youths and girls to be trundled around to their various readers.

The shops were opening. The early buses were grinding down the streets. Things were definitely moving.

Some of the elderly citizenry were up and about; the retired men and women whose lives were empty other than with deliberately self-organised habits. To rise early. To walk two miles before breakfast. To exercise an old and reluctant dog. To drive an electric wheelchair to the newspaper stall and back. To meet a friend, as if by accident, and exchange opinions about what has hap-pened in the world during the past twenty-four hours. A thousand-and-one carefully worked out routines with which to fill otherwise empty lives. To work like hell, killing the boredom which comes with the end of a working life.

Hunt paused long enough to reflect upon this as he waited at traffic lights on the outskirts of Easedale on his way to Gauntley.

Soon, within the next three years, he'd pass the age when the rules demanded that an annual medical determined whether or not he was still going to be a copper. A slightly dicky heart. A touch of asthma. The hint of arthritic joints. Such little ailments – ailments which were part of natural ageing rather than real disease – and he'd be out on a pension. A good pension, of course. It wasn't that he'd be strapped. But by Christ, he'd be bored.

Bobbying. Policing. Time was, when he'd first joined, when it was a comparatively simple, straightforward job. An up-and-down, black-and-white number. The cops versus the villains. But not for the past ten years or so. Every damned solicitor had his own tame funny farmer. Coppers were bastards. They were the Fuzz, the Pigs, the Filth. Shove an earring through one lobe, thread a safety-pin into one nostril, wear rainbow-coloured hair, bloody great medallions on dog chains, torn jeans, ripped shirts and expensive trainers . . . after that, forget the word guilty.

That's what the cops were up against. That's what made the whole exercise a waste of time. Prats who should have been drowned at birth were allowed to run wild, just because one in a hundred might – just *might* – be convicted of outlawry he hadn't actually committed. Not a nice guy. Not a good guy. Just that . . .

That was why the force – every force – was undermanned. That was why you worked your balls off, but got nowhere. That's what bobbying had become.

But what the hell else, it wasn't boring. It created ulcers, it brought on nervous breakdowns, it smashed marriages and it gave a perpetual state of screaming hab-dabs, but it wasn't boring.

Whereas retirement . . .

As the traffic lights flicked from red to red-and-amber, Hunt realised that he had no friends.

It came as quite a shock. Acquaintances by the score. Men who were his colleagues by the ton. But nobody to whom he could turn, and say, 'This is somebody special. Somebody unique. Somebody I will never let down and who, in turn, will never let me down.'

54

Maybe with Victoria, his wife. But Vic had been something quite out of the ordinary. Early, when he'd first known her, she'd laughed, where other men and woman might have quaked a little. Never – not for one moment – had she been even intimidated, much less afraid, when he'd blown his top. Maybe that's why he'd fallen in love with her . . . as much as he could fall in love with anybody.

Edward? Hell's teeth, yes! He'd wanted Edward to be close. He'd wanted the relationship to be the perfect father-son set-up. Something great. Something indestructible. But Edward had screwed things rotten by putting that silly cow, Ethel, in the family way. Then marrying her. Doing the 'right thing', instead of telling her to take a flying leap into obscurity. And then there hadn't been a child . . . only something capable of being flushed down the toilet.

Green shone on its own, and Hunt released the clutch as he eased down on the accelerator.

After the miscarriage things had gone from bad to worse. Too much work. Too short a fuse. Occasionally an almighty booze-up in an attempt to crawl from under, if only for a moment.

Then Vic had died . . .

At which point, Hunt almost died.

It was later estimated that the gravel lorry was lightly over-loaded. It was known that the road had a one-in-eight descent to the cross-roads. The driver admitted to trying to beat the lights and the vehicle examiners found that the brakes were ridiculously inadequate for the combined speed and load.

A ten-foot-high wall of steel, glass and stone chippings hit the offside of Hunt's car at a little more than fifty miles an hour. The impression was that the lorry seemed to jump up and pounce on top of the smaller vehicle. Hunt saw what was going to happen a split second before the collision. There wasn't a thing he could do. He had not time even to yell.

The car was a complete write-off. For almost a week the

medics fought to prevent Hunt, himself, from being as done for as the car.

Eventually he was moved from the Intensive Care Unit of Beechwood Brook Cottage Hospital, and those who had worked to perform something of a miracle relaxed. One arm would be almost three inches shorter than its mate, four ribs had to mend themselves, a total of more than a hundred stitches were holding various lips of torn flesh together, and there was a fair-to-middling chance that he would never walk with ease again.

But, as the Assistant Chief Constable was heard to remark, 'He always was a remarkably lucky sod.'

PART TWO
Lyle's Case

I

So what makes Rogate-on-Sands so special? What in hell do I owe the place? The only thing it has ever given me is anguish and heartbreak. At various times, it has dumped very messy problems into my lap; problems which I have had to clean up, despite a certain amount of petty vindictiveness from Crosbie. Crosbie, of course, out-pips me by one small rung of the ranking ladder – he carries a chief superintendent's clout, while I carry the slightly lesser rank of superintendent; he is uniform branch and divisional officer, I am CID and divisional detective boss man, therefore on paper he can push my nose out of any can I might decide to sniff into. On paper.

In practice, and because the force does not run to exotica like detective chief superintendents, I enjoy the status of Big Bwana in the plain clothes branch. This, of course, gives *me* clout and I can, in certain circumstances, dump Crosbie back on his fanny.

Over the years we have reached a working agreement: I hate him and he hates me. We both know just where we stand.

Why, then, did I hesitate when the strange assistant chief constable offered me a temporary respite from the hassle? Why did I ask so many unnecessary questions?

'The chief knows about this?'

'Of course.'

'What you're asking me to do?'

'Certainly.'

'And he doesn't object?'

'Lyle, I would not be here, putting the proposition to you, without his blessing.'

'Quite.' I nodded reflectively.

I sipped at my coffee, stared from the sand-specked window of The Pier-End Snackery and watched the off-white horses ride towards the prom on the curl of some very muddy-looking waves.

For some stupid reason I said, 'That sea. Look at it.'

'What about it?' The tone was curt and puzzled.

'The colour,' I explained. 'The colour of grubby, khaki, battledress. It isn't sea any more. It's thin slush. Filthy slush.'

'I can't see what—'

'People come here for a holiday. For the sunshine. For the sea. For the sand. It's rather like holidaying at a sewage farm, but they can't see it.'

'The world is full of mugs, Superintendent.' The tone was that of a man jollying along some mildly pixilated nut. He added, 'Now. About your taking on the Tabitha Wardle enquiry.'

'There's no chance of Hunt picking up the reins again?' I asked.

'He's finished,' said the ACC bluntly. 'The wonder is the car crash didn't kill him. His policing days are over.'

'Somebody else?' I suggested. '*Somebody* must have been steering the ship, since Hunt was knocked into the hospital.'

'Not to mean much.' The Assistant Chief Constable hesitated, then said, 'You want the truth?'

'If I don't get it, you've had a wasted journey.'

'It's a personal opinion, but I'll lay my life I'm not far wrong.'

'And?'

'Hunt was never the whizz-kid he was cracked up to be. The whizz-kid he, himself, claimed to be. He tried to frighten people. That was his way of "detecting" crime. The bish-bash-bosh method. Sometimes it just didn't work.'

'Sometimes,' I murmured. 'On the other hand . . . *sometimes*.'

In the distance, a kid was walking along the prom. He was kicking a coloured football. People were having to swerve to avoid him. One guy had to duck. At a pinch, the kid was being a bloody nuisance.

The ACC said, 'You've earned yourself a reputation.'

'Have I?'

'Don't be coy, Lyle. If you were just another run-of-the-mill jack, I wouldn't be here.'

Somebody tapped the football back to the boy's feet. The kid made a full-blooded kick at it, sliced the kick and the ball sailed over the promenade railings and into the sea. At a guess, only the kid was disappointed.

The ACC said, 'It wouldn't be the first time you've been seconded. You – er – seem to have been in demand, at various times.'

'I've been lucky,' I grunted, then sipped the coffee.

'Why not be "lucky" with us?'

'First of August,' I said gently.

'Eh?'

'It's now mid-October. The body's dead and buried. The clues – if there *were* clues – are cold and blown away. What the hell!'

'Give it a try.' He was almost pleading.

I asked what was to me an obvious question. 'Why not Scotland Yard?'

'They wouldn't touch it after this time lag.'

'With instructions from the Home Secretary,' I said.

'Perhaps.'

'Why not an official request?'

'Lyle.' He cleared his throat. What he was saying took some dragging out. 'We're provincial. One of the "North of Watford" forces. They'd crow.'

'Oh, come *on*.'

'You know damned well,' he growled. 'They'd do things *their* way—'

'Of course.'

'—and that might mean some stupid, great upheaval. Mass fingerprinting . . . something like that.'

'And if something like that happens to be necessary?'

'We have a very cash-conscious Police Authority.'

'Oh, for Christ's sake!'

61

'Man, you don't know.' The tone had the hint of a moaning quality. 'You've no idea. They want a Rolls for the price of a Mini. It's just not possible.'

'Which is where I come in,' I grunted. 'I'm the Mini, tarted up as a Rolls.'

'Look, I don't want you to—'

'I'll get re-fills,' I interrupted.

I stood up from the table. Squashed out what was left of my cigarette, then carried the cups back to the counter and ordered fresh coffee.

The Pier-End Snackery had the usual end-of-season scratches and bruises. Even a place like Rogate-on-Sands gets the occasional lout. The counter – like some of the tables – had chips on the formica-topped surface. Chips and cigarette burns. The glass of one of the display cabinets was cracked. Despite being scrubbed, rude graffiti showed, ghost-like, in a corner of one of the walls; come next season a redecorating job would smarten everything up, but meanwhile the attempt at 'olde worlde' class and comfort had been ruined.

A gust of wind threw more sand particles at the glass of the windows as I returned to my seat. I placed the new cups of coffee into position, seated myself and spooned sugar into my own drink before I spoke.

I said, 'What sort of arrangements have been made, as far as accommodation's concerned?'

'Bed and breakfast, at the Thatched Oak.'

'A pub?'

'An inn, actually. Seventeenth century, so I'm told. Bathroom en suite. Good nosh. I think you'll find it comfortable.'

'Near – where is it? – Easedale?'

'That's the section. But the Thatched Oak is on the outskirts of Gauntley itself. Make it your headquarters. We've had a word with the landlord. He has no objections.'

'You seem to have taken a lot for granted,' I observed.

'We were hopeful.'

I sipped some more coffee. I lighted a second cigarette. I tried to think out valid reasons for telling Calfordshire

Constabulary to take a running jump.

The ACC waited, and watched my face.

'When would I be expected to start?' I asked.

'As soon as possible.' He gave a quick, half-smile and added, 'Tomorrow?'

'I'd need a Man Friday. Somebody who knows as much about the case as possible.'

'Detective Sergeant Moody. He's young. He's ambitious. He was at the scene that same night. He even has passing knowledge of the village, and those who live there.'

'Fine.' I nodded. Without me formally accepting the job – without the ACC formally acknowledging my acceptance – it was already an understood thing. I said, 'The files, the statements, the photographs – all the paperwork – I'll want access to that, of course.'

'It's ready and waiting. We can have it at the Thatched Oak, if you'd prefer it that way.'

'It might be nice,' I agreed. 'It might make interesting bed-time reading.'

II

The ACC had been right.

The ACC's name was Needham. A good, old-fashioned North Country name which seemed to carry with it a promise of down-to-earth honesty. And he'd been honest enough about the Thatched Oak . . . it *was* thatched. It had a polished-floor restaurant, complete with oak beams and a massive inglenook fireplace. It had a correspondingly large fire-basket, which was well filled and, with that blaze, central heating was superfluous. It was warm, comfortable, and a delightful counter to the first frosts of the year.

The meal had been one the like of which I hadn't tasted for months. Soup, which hadn't even seen a can. Honest to God roast beef, but of Scotland rather than old England; Aberdeen Angus, for sure, and spit-roasted the old-fashioned way. Yorkshire pudding – what we used to call bun puddings, light as thistledown and a perfect

63

companion to the beef. Roast potatoes, creamed potatoes, sprouts, cauliflower and baby carrots spread with thick, onion-heavy gravy. And the flavouring of horseradish sauce on the lips of the plate. A glass of ice-cold scrumpy to add a bite to the taste. And for 'afters' home-made apple pie with whipped cream.

It had been a feast for the Gods, and now I was finishing it off with fine coffee, cracker biscuits and good cheese.

I had arrived at the Thatched Oak that early evening; the day the ACC had visited Rogate-on-Sands; twenty-four hours before I was expected at Gauntley. I figured it to be a wise move. A testing of the water, before plunging in head-first.

And (as I've already mentioned) Needham had been so right. The inn was something straight from a romantic water colour. White walled, with a beetling overhang of thatch; small windowed, with ivy and wistaria touching the upper sills. Inside, there was a solid, beeswax cleanliness and if, here and there, boards or stairs creaked, it was the creak of fine timber, thoroughly seasoned and still 'alive' enough to spring with the weight of whoever walked over it.

Alongside where I was sitting, the tiny-paned window gave the appearance of a set of black mirrors. When I'd first entered the room I'd been able to see the country garden effect of the inn's surround, but since the dozens of low-powered wall lights had been switched on the outside world had disappeared.

The waiters and waitresses were uniformed in mock-Eton jackets – the old 'bum-freezers' – and they looked above-average smart. One of them swanned nearer, gave a tiny half-bow and asked a very civilised question.

'Everything to your satisfaction, sir?'

'Fine.'

'Cigar, sir?'

He held out a small, compartmentalised tray, but I shook my head.

'I poison myself on cigarettes,' I smiled, then added, 'What's it like outside?'

'Cool, but dry.'

'Good. I'll have a quiet stroll before I turn in.'

I finished the cheese and biscuits, drained the coffee cup and felt particularly self-congratulatory by refraining from lighting a cigarette. I called at the tiny cloakroom behind the reception desk and picked up my lightweight mac against the October chill. Then I strolled outside and enjoyed a few first breaths of cool, autumnal air.

It was different from the sea-tanged air of Rogate-on-Sands. There was the hint of garden bonfire. There was a touch of farmyard tang. It was clean. It was clear. It made its way into the lungs with all the sweet purity of iced champagne.

I walked about twenty yards along the gravel path which sliced across the inn's lawned and bordered gardens. The noise from the inn faded into the background and, for a moment or two, I congratulated myself on my good fortune in building up a small reputation as a man capable of interviewing the truth from his fellow men. I stood there and, in a roundabout way, sympathised with unfortunates whose professions stripped them of the capacity to wonder; who earned their livelihood performing mundane, soul-destroying acts. I breathed in the air and fought against another wave of temptation to light up a cigarette.

A voice said, 'Mr Lyle?'

It startled me a little. It was a young voice – a woman's voice – and its owner had approached noiselessly across the turf of the lawn.

I turned and said, 'That's my name.'

'I'm sorry.' She was still in her teens, and she was having difficulty in expressing herself. She said, 'My name's Madge. Madge Wardle.'

'Hello, Madge Wardle,' I smiled.

I turned and side-by-side we walked slowly back towards the inn.

She said, 'Mr Moody said you were coming.'

'Mr Moody?'

'Detective Sergeant Moody.'

'Oh.'

'And Milly Wallace told me you'd arrived.'

65

'Milly Wallace?'

'The landlord's wife.'

'Ah.'

'We both use the same hairdresser.'

'That follows,' I said drily.

'And I had to see you.'

'Of course.'

'As soon as possible.'

'Naturally.'

She took a breath, and said, 'If it's Alex ... don't do anything. Please.'

'Alex?'

'Alex Wardle. My father.'

We were almost back at the entrance to the inn. Tables and chairs, placed for outdoor drinking and refreshment, were still in place on a flagged patio.

I said, 'Do you drink?' Then, as an afterthought I added, 'Are you *old* enough to drink?'

'I'm old enough. I just don't like the taste.'

'Good sense.' I steered her towards one of the table-and-chair sets. 'Let's sit for a while. If it's not too chilly.'

'I'd like that.'

We sat opposite each other at one of the tables. I allowed my good resolutions to go down the john and fished cigarettes and a lighter from my pocket.

She said, 'I'd like one of those, please.' A quick smile made her face change into a countenance of pure happiness, as she added, 'I'm old enough to smoke.'

'That is *not* good sense.' Nevertheless, I lighted two of the cigarettes and handed one across the table. Then I said, 'We are, of course, talking about the murder of Tabitha Wardle.'

'Tabs.' She drew in a deep, lung-filling inhalation.

'Your mother?'

'Yes.'

'Alex being your father? PC Wardle?'

'Yes.'

'And you think your father might be the person who shot your mother?'

66

'Of course.'

I pulled on the cigarette, then in a soft voice asked, 'Why "of course"?'

'He had reasons enough.'

'Motive, you mean?'

'Yes. Motive and to spare.'

I allowed her answer to hang in the evening air for a few moments, then in a gentle, parental voice said, 'What did she do that was motive enough for murder?'

'I don't like the word.'

'Which word?'

'Murder.'

'What would *you* call it?'

'Killing. He killed her. He's only human. He can't be blamed . . . not really.'

'The law might not agree,' I murmured.

'You can't *really* blame him,' she insisted.

'Okay.' I took another draw on the cigarette, then said, 'Tell me why we can't blame him.'

'He was patient. Very patient.'

'And?'

'There's a limit. There's a limit to everything.'

'And she over-stepped the limit?' I teased.

'She couldn't help it. It's a form of illness.'

'What was the nature of her illness?'

'You'll . . .' She waved the cigarette in the air a little. 'Y'know . . . you'll be seeing Doctor Harrison?'

'Of course. Eventually.'

'He'll tell you. It *was* an illness.'

'You've already said.'

'Damn!' Coming from her, the tiny swear-word sounded like an obscenity. 'She was almost strait-laced. They won't say that, but she *was*.'

' "They"?'

'The villagers. Those who guessed. They make it sound like she was a whore. But she wasn't.'

'She wasn't a whore?' It was an oblique question. But why not? I was feeling my way, and not wanting to scare this young lady into silence.

67

'Of course she wasn't.' There was ready anger there. Defensive anger. She added, 'Ask Doctor Harrison.'

'Sure.' I nodded. I almost blew it, when I observed, 'Some people flirt. They can't help themselves.'

'Not flirting. Not just *that*.'

'No?'

'She wouldn't have hurt Alex by *flirting*. She wouldn't, anyway. She wasn't the sort.'

'I'm sorry, but—'

'You're like the rest.' She was suddenly very angry. She squashed out her cigarette in the table's ash-tray. She almost spat the word, 'Men.'

'I'm a man,' I admitted.

'If it's satyriasis, that's fine. Something to be proud of. Something to brag about. *That's* not an illness. Oh, my word no.'

She stood up and turned to go.

'Look . . .' I began. But it was too late. She didn't hear. She didn't want to listen. She flounced away, across the patio, along the path and into the gloom.

I watched her go, and felt a little sad. I liked her – I liked her kind – and Police Constable Wardle was a lucky man. He had a daughter, convinced of his guilt but ready to plead for him from the off.

III

Moody checked that all the bits and pieces were geometrically correct on the surface of the table-desk Needham had sent out to the Thatched Oak from Calfordshire Constabulary Stores. He checked that the pencils were all sharpened, checked that the blotting-paper was firmly cornered in its holder and checked that the drawers, down one side of the desk, moved smoothly on their runners.

Meanwhile, I sat in a surprisingly comfortable bedroom easy chair and glanced through the Initial Incident Report, Medical Report and Post-Mortem Report.

I'd met Detective Sergeant Moody at breakfast, a couple of hours before.

I'd slept well, thanks to a double whisky and a good bed, and had been awakened by one of the staff, bringing me early morning tea and the day's newspaper. I'd showered and shaved in the en suite bathroom, then I'd dressed and wandered downstairs to the dining room. Fruit juice, followed by kippers had made a pleasant change from the usual frugal, lift-it-from-the-fridge-and-eat-it breakfast with which I normally started my day.

As I'd started to spread marmalade onto the first piece of toast Detective Sergeant Moody had entered the dining room and introduced himself. He had (he told me) accompanied a van from force headquarters, bringing the paperwork covering the Tabitha Wardle murder, and also a desk, a filing cabinet, a typewriter and all the various paraphernalia Needham figured I needed in order to perform the function of 'outside expert'.

He'd stood a little awkwardly alongside the table after he'd introduced himself, and I'd waved an arm and said, 'Take a seat. Coffee?'

'Thank you, sir.'

'Toast? Marmalade?'

'Thank you, sir.' The idea of almost breakfasting with me seemed to relax him a little. He said, 'The ACC said I had to fix whatever you required.'

'I'll let you know,' I promised.

As we'd eaten together, I'd asked him about the murdered woman, Tabitha Wardle.

The way he answered the questions – the way he chose the words with care – showed his determination not to express a biased view.

'You knew her,' I'd pressed. It had been a statement; a reminder rather than a question.

'A little,' he'd admitted.

'Rather more than a little, surely?'

'I knew Wardle – *know* Wardle – PC Wardle.'

'Wardle, but not his wife?'

'Wardle's an Easedale officer. Like me.'

69

'But not his wife?' I'd insisted.

'I knew her. Of course I knew her. By sight, enough to pass the time of day, perhaps. I knew – I knew of her reputation. I'd heard of her reputation.'

'She had a "reputation"?' I'd pretended surprise.

'She was a tease. That's what I've heard. *Had* heard.'

'A tease?'

'A bit – y'know – hot.'

'Hot?' I played it dumb. I wanted him to commit himself.

'Y'know . . .' He'd floundered.

'Hot *arsed*?'

'That's – that's what they say.'

'Who?'

'Eh?'

'Who says she was hot arsed?'

'Sir.' He'd swallowed, then muttered, 'Sir, I try to deal in facts. I try not to—'

'That's a fact,' I'd interrupted.

'Sir?'

'The late Tabitha Wardle's backside. Whether she was or wasn't given to fornicatory gymnastics, without too much encouragement. Facts, Sergeant. Facts that might even add up to a possible motive. Do I make sense?'

'Yes, sir. Of course, sir. Of *course*.'

It had, of course, been something of a try-on. I wanted this young copper to fully appreciate that I was quite shock-proof. I wanted a colleague. I didn't want an out-ranked yes-man.

We'd sipped coffee and we'd chatted. We'd allowed our respective personalities to sniff around each other. Then we'd eased the tension a little; slipped the odd swear word in now and then; narrowed the gulf between the two ranks until, while still being there, it was hardly noticeable.

Then we'd left the dining room and come upstairs to the bedroom. The officers who'd delivered the equipment had done a neat job, and while Moody checked that everything functioned, I glanced through the first documents on the file.

70

I said, 'It was a hot day. The day before the murder – a particularly hot day.'

'A hot day,' he agreed. He repositioned the desk clock slightly, and added, 'It was also a hot night.'

'Hot,' I repeated. I made it a throwaway remark, as I added, 'Hot enough not to be wearing much. A thin dress and a pair of shoes. No underclothes.'

'It was very hot.' He either didn't understand or refused to be drawn. He said, 'No footprints. No tyre marks. The earth was as hard as concrete.'

I flicked a page and said, 'She was shot from close range. The cartridge wad was found in her chest cavity.'

'What was left of it.' He lowered himself onto the bottom corner of the bed. 'I've read and re-read those documents, sir. Estimated distance between the barrel and her front, six-to-eight feet. Standard twelve-bore. Both barrels. That's what the boffins say. I believe 'em. I saw her. It damn near took her off, just below the shoulders.'

His lips tightened and his nostrils flared for a moment as the memory returned.

'Her husband found her,' I observed.

'Constable Wardle. He was on duty . . . that's why he found her.'

'Is it?'

'A place called Hangman's Lane.'

'Ah, yes. Hangman's Lane. Why, I wonder?'

'Why?' He looked puzzled.

'Why Hangman's Lane?' I expanded. 'I've glanced at the plan drawing. No houses. No lock-up property. Nothing. Close to midnight. It doesn't lead anywhere. So, why Hangman's Lane?'

'It's part of his beat.' He knew it was a remarkably lame excuse, and added, 'I see what you're getting at. But it *is* part of Gauntley Beat.'

I eyed him with a certain amount of silent contempt.

He coloured slightly, then said, 'The patrol sergeant was with him. Maybe they heard something. Saw something.'

'The gunshot?' I suggested.

'It's – y'know it's possible.'

'Any mention of that possibility in his statement?'

'Sergeant Poole's statement?'

'His. Or Wardle's own statement come to that.'

'No.' He shook his head and continued to look uncomfortable. He said, 'When Chief Superintendent Hunt was injured things were knocked sideways. A lot of loose ends were left dangling. Nobody there to co-ordinate things.'

'Who took the statements?'

'Sir?'

'From Wardle. From this Sergeant Poole. Who took their statements?'

'Er – I did, sir.'

'Therefore?'

I allowed the criticism which rode the one-word question to sink in. Moody knew what I was getting at and it ruffled him a little.

He said, 'There was something of a turmoil, sir. When—'

'I know "when",' I snapped. 'The message *I'm* getting is that this is a one-man force. Remove that man – and forget down-to-earth bobbying.'

'No, sir. Just that we're a remarkably friendly force. We all—'

'That means a remarkably incompetent force, Sergeant.'

'Sir?'

'That expression. "Friendly". A brainless expression. Those we're up against – the bastards – they hate us. If we're any good, they hate us. That's as it should be.'

'Sir, I'm talking about—'

'*I'm* talking about *murder*. Unsolved. No suspects. No leads. I'm talking about everybody. You, me, Wardle, Poole . . . every man, woman and child within travelling distance of Hangman's Lane. We are not playing footsie, Sergeant Moody. We're playing Hunt the Murderer. It's a serious game and we are – supposedly – professionals.'

'Yes, sir.' He was subdued. And that, too, was as it should be.

I finished, 'Arrange for Poole to be available for a

prolonged interview this afternoon. Meanwhile, you and I will take a short trip to Hangman's Lane and see what's left of the scene.'

IV

The two rowan trees, standing one at each side of the entrance to Hangman's Lane were, perhaps, symbolic. To oldsters, the rowan was bad luck; it stood for heartache and suffering – even death – and that, too, was as it should be.

The crime was murder; the theft of life; the removal of a human being from the face of the planet. I'd handled murder hunts before. Maybe more than my fair share. And for those who wish to be let into a secret, let me give a solemn assurance. Murder is in a league apart. It carries its own weight of frightfulness. Not too long ago its detection equated with two deaths. At least two deaths. The death of the victim and the death of the criminal responsible for that death. Maybe that was a good thing – maybe it was one of the few pure and uncomplicated laws we've ever had: on the other hand, maybe not. Maybe we've become more civilised.

Coppers, of course, should not think those thoughts. Coppers are required to be objective. Very objective. Every book of words about policing lays great stress upon the complete objectivity of every good copper, and every time that load of crap about objectivity comes up I want to puke.

Who the hell can be objective at a funeral? Consult the nearest mourners. Ask them about objectivity.

So with murder. So with a murder enquiry. We don't kill them these days. We bury them alive. Twenty-five years, twenty years, even ten years . . . it sounds nothing to those who do not have it to work. But ask around. Ask those who have suffered even one or two years.

Whatever he or she was when the doors were opened to admit them, when the doors are opened to release them,

73

what comes out is a terrified animal.

I'd seen too many. I knew the end product. It follows that I was not feeling too frisky as I drove the car along Hangman's Lane.

Moody told me where to stop. He led me to a gate, opened it and led me into a field.

He pointed to a hedge bottom, then had some difficulty in speaking.

'That's – y'know . . . She was there.'

'When you got here? When you first arrived?'

'Yeah.' The word could hardly be heard. He was remembering things he didn't enjoy remembering.

The hedge was the usual hawthorn growing through and around a broken-down post and rail core. At some time in the season the outside of the hedge had been trimmed, but now – like a man badly in need of a shave – it was growing ragged.

I stared at the scene for a few moments before I spoke again.

I observed, 'Not a very usual field. Forty feet wide, thereabout. Two hundred yards long, again thereabouts.'

'The strip business,' he growled.

'Strip?'

'Old-fashioned. Mediaeval. The strip-farming method of agriculture. The remnants can still be found.'

'Like here?'

'That's what this is. Some of the locals use it for whippet racing. Sometimes – not often – the caravan people camp in here.'

'Gypsies?'

'Not really. Tinkers, really. Travellers.'

'No distance at all.' I glanced first to my right, then to my left. 'From the gate to where she was found. No distance at all.'

'People come in here.' He spoke in a low voice. 'Couples, seeking privacy. Courting couples. It's a sort of – a sort of . . .'

He dried up. The emotion was getting to be too much for him.

I waited. I watched his face as it mirrored his feelings; as he stared at the place where the murdered woman must have been standing when the shot hit her.

He muttered, 'She was – y'know – *there*. Both – both barrels. In the chest. It was . . . some of it went *through* her. It was awful.'

'The gate.' I forced his attention away from the spot he was gazing at. 'It was open?'

'Yes.' He nodded. 'When we arrived. When I arrived. When I arrived. It was ajar. Not wide open, but ajar. Wardle had been in, of course. So had Poole. It may – y'know – it may have been closed when *they* arrived, but the gate was ajar when *I* arrived.'

'Hunt didn't see the body?'

'No. He was on his way here when—'

'Therefore, whatever opinion he gives – gave – is suspect?'

'Sir, he is a chief superintendent. He has a mass of experience – from which he can—'

'The only thing he did,' I insisted. 'The only thing he *could* do, was to guide everybody through the overture. The opera itself – the part that mattered – was played out without a conductor . . . figuratively speaking.'

'Yeah. I – er – I suppose so.'

Without consciously making a decision to leave the scene we made our way back to the gate. As he closed it the hinges dropped, with the gate still almost two feet from the closed position. He had to lift it above the grass and soil for the last couple of feet.

We glanced at each other as he fastened the chain. We both knew the chances were that the gate was ajar when Poole and Wardle arrived on the night of the murder.

V

Lunch was cheese and tomato quiche, with salad garnish, coleslaw and granary bread. I chewed it slowly, savouring the taste, and cleansing my mouth with a dry Muscadet

Sevre et Maine. The wine was wrong for the connoisseurs, but who cared? Which connoisseur was likely to order cheese and tomato quiche, anyway? And it was my taste buds which were enjoying themselves.

The waiter, the guy who'd offered me a cigar the previous evening, was again on duty and by this time some of the barriers were down, and to a limited degree we could exchange pleasantries.

It helped that I was only one of three guests staying at the Thatched Oak. It helped even more than the other two were obviously in their dotage and embarrassing everybody by performing a never-ending version of geriatric Romeo and Juliet with each other.

The waiter stood alongside the table and murmured, 'Am I allowed to ask how your enquiry is progressing, sir?'

'You may ask,' I said. 'The answer is, "I am, at the moment, familiarising myself with the basic facts." Which, of course, means very little.'

'We are a tight-knit community, sir.'

'So I've gathered.'

'Constable Wardle's wife was well known in the village.'

'A tight-knit community . . . a very small community.'

'Just so, sir.'

'You live in Gauntley?' I asked.

'All my life, sir.'

'Unusual,' I remarked.

'Sir?'

'Waiters. Hotel staff. In the main, itinerant workers . . . that's my impression.'

'In the main,' he agreed. 'For myself, I have an invalid sister. We have no other relations. I am perfectly happy to live at home and work at the Thatched Oak. I consider myself a fortunate man.'

A few tables away the grey-haired Lothario grinned at his lady-love and placed a hand on her knee.

The waiter noticed my slightly raised eyebrow, turned his head, glanced, allowed what might have been taken as a quick smile to touch his lips and murmured, 'They're on their honeymoon, sir.'

My brow went a shade higher as I said, 'What's that? An empty boast? A ridiculous claim? Or an unacceptable excuse?'

'They're happy, sir.' There was a hint of criticism in his tone.

I chewed a mouthful of quiche and salad, swallowed and sipped wine before I spoke again.

I said, 'Tell me about Gauntley.'

He hesitated for a second, then said, 'Not for the record, sir.'

'For my personal information. To fill in the background. No more than that.'

'The usual rural community, sir. Cliques. Extended families. Loves and hatreds. Likes and dislikes. There's nothing unusual here, sir. Scratch the surface of any English village and you'll find another Gauntley.'

'Complete with murder?' I mocked.

'Complete with a *will* to murder. Complete with enough jealousy – enough unjustified malice – to trigger off a dozen murders.'

'There is,' I murmured, 'more to rusticity than meets the eye.'

'Not all Morris Dancing and maypoles,' he smiled.

The honeymoon couple had moved to the whispering-sweet-nothings-into-the-other's-ear stage. It was difficult not to seem to watch, but who the hell wanted to play Peeping Tom on such ancient tomfoolery.

Merely in order to say something, I asked, 'Okay, villages usually have top families. The squire. The main landowner. That sort of thing. What about Gauntley?'

'No squire, sir. No main landowner . . . not really. Three main farmers, but they're all working farmers. None of them have time to worry about whatever's happening other than on their own land. We have Charlie Calverley, of course. *He* still lives here.'

'Charlie Calverley?'

'The comedian. He was once—'

'I know who Charlie Calverley is. The fact is, I thought he was dead and buried.'

77

'No, sir. He's lived here for the last twenty years, thereabouts. He's been retired for almost ten of those years.'

'I'll be damned!'

'He takes a very paternal interest in the village.'

'That means he'll know—'

'He knows just about everything, sir. He makes it his business to know what's going on in the village.'

'Good.' I smiled. 'Things are looking up.'

'He'll, er . . .' He looked uncomfortable, then closed his mouth.

'Something I should know?' I queried.

'He's, y'know . . . awkward.'

'Is he?'

'He has a reputation, I'm afraid.'

'A reputation?'

'He clams up, if people ask too many questions.'

'Does he, indeed?'

'He enjoys being domineering. That's the truth of it.'

'Uhuh.' I dropped my voice into the deep freeze compartment, and said, 'Charlie Calverley is renowned for telling funny stories. *I'm* not. But, bet money on it, he'll tell *me* the stories I want him to tell me . . . and they won't even be worth a smile.'

The antediluvian love birds hoisted themselves from their seats and shuffled from the dining room. They hobbled along, side-by-side, with their little fingers linked, like two grey-haired teenagers out on their first date.

We had the dining room to ourselves, and I said, 'Okay, you're not Charlie Calverley, but you've lived here long enough to have opinions. Who do you think killed her?'

The answer was a gentle smile, laced with a certain 'knowing' quality.

'You're probably wrong, of course.' I sipped the wine and watched his face. 'You're biased. Everybody's biased – one way or the other – on a subject like murder. But your opinion might be interesting.'

'Ask me about . . .' He moved a finger in a tiny gesture. 'About the wine you're drinking. About the degree of comfort offered by the Thatched Oak. About the expertise of those who work in the kitchen. I have opinions. If pressed, I might voice those opinions. But about murder . . . no, Superintendent Lyle.'

'You were interested enough,' I growled. 'You asked.'

'Morbidity, sir.' He kept a very po-faced expression in place. 'A natural interest. When Sergeant Moody mentioned your reason for visiting the village we were all somewhat curious, naturally.'

'Naturally.'

'We – er . . .' He made soft, polite throat-clearing noises. 'Forgive me for being rather blunt, Superintendent.'

'Be blunt,' I invited.

'We do not wish you success. It would be a pity.'

'Is that a fact?'

'A little unjust, perhaps.'

'I deal in law. I leave "justice" to those who figure themselves as God.'

'We think—'

'We?' I interrupted.

'The village. The majority of the villagers. We think Constable Wardle deserves more than the strict law can offer.'

VI

I drove into Easedale at a very steady rate of knots. I wanted time to think and I wanted to iron out a few bends and wrinkles in what I'd figured to be a moderately straightforward killing enquiry.

The time scale had perhaps thrown me. A gap of around twelve weeks – from the first day of August to mid-October – was a difficult period to bridge. Not yet criminal history, but one hell of a way from hot news. The shock had had time to wear off. The outrage and the indignation had had time to cool. Because the Wardle woman had been iced, no longer equated with her being purer than clinical linen. What she *really* was was showing through. Her once-upon-a-time priceless virtues were becoming slightly tarnished.

Her own daughter had left me in little doubt. The waiter had wandered close to the subject, then veered away like a startled colt. Tabitha Wardle had, it would seem, made enemies. Not just people who didn't like her. People who admitted to no real surprise at her violent death. People who should be professing a natural love for her, but who were in fact admitting something not too far short of loathing.

It shunted the possibilities around a little; blurred the edges which, in the normal course of events, limited the reasonable probabilities as far as suspects were concerned. In this one, anything was possible. Anything was probable . . . it really was anybody's fouled up baby.

Interlude

The murderer couldn't help worrying.

At first – a small lifetime ago – he'd been ready to give himself up. To put himself on trial. To plead guilty. At that moment he was ready, and no price was too high. The squeeze of the trigger, the tiny jump of the shotgun in his hands as the twin hammers fell, the explosion of blood, bone and tissue of what had, a shaved second earlier, been Tabs.

Then the great surge of self-disgust and the breathless drowning in a sea of sudden guilt.

That was it. That was the moment. Come that first full day – that first Wednesday – and the killing would not have required any enquiry. It would not have required detecting. Come daylight – come a decent hour – and he'd have given himself up. Indeed, giving himself up had, perhaps only sub-consciously, been part of the plan.

Then Hunt had been smashed into mere insignificance.

It had been a little like being strangled, then at the last moment being allowed to breathe. Like being slammed inside a cell, then discovering that the cell door had been left unlocked.

The relief had made for a certain, temporary light-headedness. Then reality had returned and, with it, the realisation that a confession would do nobody any good.

Hunt was no longer around. And – as he discovered – Hunt was the man the murderer feared. Hunt might have bulldozed his way to the truth, but if not Hunt, nobody. And as the weeks had passed, the feeling of safety had grown. He'd got away with the big one. With murder. All he had to do now was to keep his head down, keep his mouth shut and keep his wits about him.

Until this man Lyle arrived on the scene.

Who the hell was Lyle? What sort of a reputation had he? Why Lyle? Why not the Met? Why, and if necessary, not some Assistant Chief Constable? Why only a Superintendent?

So many questions. So few answers.

The murderer was worried, and the murderer was seeking some sort of information . . . if possible.

83

VII

Easedale nick was a dismal, soulless place. It hadn't been built as a police station, and it showed. In the first place it was three storeys high and, if the grilles set in the pavement surround told a true tale, it also had cellars. And this, for Christ's sake, for only a section station. Before I walked inside, I knew one of its main faults: too many rooms, and few of them large enough for convenient policing.

The guy with buttons, doing duty at the public counter, told me where the CID office was. I didn't know him. He didn't know me. It made no difference . . . that was the degree of security in the dump.

At the top of the first flight of stairs, just as I duly turned right for the CID office, I almost bumped into a stranger. He was friendly enough. He nodded and smiled a greeting in passing. He seemed to know me. If so, he had the advantage . . . I didn't know *him*.

I found the CID office, found Moody waiting for me and mentioned the stranger I'd just passed.

'Inspector Mantell,' said Moody off-handedly. 'He's just left.'

'Here? This office?'

'Sure. He was interested.'

'In what?'

'The case, sir. Y'know . . . whether we'd uncovered anything fresh about the case.'

'A *detective* inspector?' I asked gently.

'No, sir. Uniformed. He doesn't always wear his uniform, though.'

'Moody.' The office door was not quite closed. I closed it very gently and very deliberately before I turned towards

85

him and continued. 'You and me. We're CID. Plain Clothes Branch. The "jacks".' I spoke slowly and softly, but he heard every word. 'This Mantell character. He is a wooden-top. One of the button boys. Uniformed. I know – don't tell me – the book of words says we should love each other. When you left the pavement-crushing crowd and started detecting crime, some mealy-mouthed bastard no doubt explained that it was only a sideways shift. It wasn't a promotion.'

'Yes, sir. That's what I was—'

'Always!' I allowed my lips to curl a little. 'The crap they feed you, Sergeant. The crap which, if you aren't careful, you swallow. But tell me. Explain, if you please. If movement from uniformed to plain clothes isn't promotion, how come, if you drop a goolie, a move back to uniform is a *de*motion? How the hell can you go down, if you haven't come up? What do they do? Dig a bloody hole?'

By this time, Moody's jaw was slack. His face was flushed and his eyes were widening and starting to glare. That was okay by me. It meant the message was getting home. It meant he was motoring down my carriageway.

I said, 'You get my gist, I hope. That CID is not a slightly flashier edition of the uniform branch. It is different. Very different. It deals with crime and *only* crime – up to and including murder. And that, Sergeant, is what we're dealing with at the moment.

'If we require men in uniform – if we *need* them – we'll make the appropriate requests. *I'll* make the request. Meanwhile, we do not – repeat *not* – discuss the case – this case or any other case – with anybody not immediately handling the case. I do hope I make myself clear.'

'Very – very clear, sir.' The words almost choked him.

'Did you tell him much?' Having roasted him, I softened my tone a little and eased him from the griddle.

'He was . . .' Moody swallowed. 'He was interested, sir. That's all.'

'I'll bet.'

'He – he said he knew you.'

86

'No way.'

'Of you. Said he knew *of* you.'

'That, too, I very much doubt.'

'I didn't know, sir.' His tone was stiff and formal. 'It won't happen again, sir.'

'That pleases me, Sergeant.' I allowed a slightly frosty smile to touch my lips. It was all play-acting, of course. It was a con and a come-on, but that was okay. Maybe that was the main reason for me being around. I said, 'Sergeant Poole?'

'He's here, sir. Waiting in the Interview Room.'

'Good.'

'He's been waiting more than a quarter of an hour.'

'Sergeant.' I lifted an eyebrow. 'Assuming *you* were the man we're after. Wouldn't fifteen minutes of quiet contemplation fray your nerves a little?'

VIII

An Interview Room should be as near to 'the truth' as it is possible to quantify that intellectual ideal. It should be without fuss. It should be clinically clean. There should be no distractions. It should not be too comfortable. There should, perhaps, be a hint of fear.

Purpose-built interview rooms are constructed with this in mind, but it is sometimes difficult to transform a room intended for more comfortable purposes into a functional Interview Room.

The Easedale Police Station Interview Room was a complete disaster. Instead of the usual simple, deal-topped table in the middle of the room, an old-fashioned, roll-topped desk, complete with a maze of pigeon-holes and drawers stood against one wall. Instead of non-patterned lino on the floor, there was an ancient carpet square; worn, a mite tattered here and there, but despite this warm-looking. There was even a fireplace complete with tiled surround and frontage and, although the grate was filled in with painted ply-board, a three-bar electric

87

fire stood on the hearth, with one of its bars glowing and sending comfortable warmth into the room. There was a swivel-chair at the desk, an office chair with arms alongside the desk and a couple more high-backed chairs positioned around the walls.

The consulting room of a particularly old-fashioned medic . . . certainly. A police station interview room . . . never.

A middle-aged man, in uniform and sporting sergeant's chevrons stood up from the swivel-chair as we entered. I waved him down, closed the door, motioned for Moody to occupy one of the high-backed chairs, out of the uniformed man's vision, then settled myself into the chair alongside the desk. I wasted a few moments pretending to get settled, while Moody crossed his legs, positioned the clipboard and foolscap we'd brought and slipped a pen from his inside pocket.

Then, I said, 'Introductions, first. My name's Lyle. Detective Superintendent Lyle.'

'Yes, sir.' His voice left no doubt. He was very tight and very proper.

'Your name is Poole,' I said.

'One-zero-one-eight, sir. Police Sergeant Percival Horace Poole.'

'As ever was,' I murmured.

'Sir?'

'Come out of the deep freeze, Sergeant. I'm here to get a clearer picture of what happened on the night of Tabitha Wardle's death. That's all.'

'Yes, sir.' If he'd relaxed at all it didn't show.

'You were there when her body was found?'

'Yes, sir.'

'Fine. Now, tell me. In your own words. Tell me what happened.'

He swallowed, and began, 'We were driving down Hangman's Lane—'

'We?'

'Constable Wardle and me.'

'Why were you with Wardle?'

'I was on duty, sir. Night shift. I was giving Wardle a company visit.'

'That will be shown in your notebook?'

'Yes, sir. Of course.'

'And in Wardle's notebook?'

'I recorded the visit in his notebook myself.'

'When and where you met? When and where you parted?'

'Yes, sir. Of course.'

'Okay, you were in Hangman's Lane . . . right?'

'Yes, sir.'

'Why?'

'Sir?'

'Why Hangman's Lane? It leads nowhere. The time was . . . what?'

'Just after twelve, sir. Twelve-fifteen . . . within a minute or so either way.'

'In the van – Wardle's police van – that's what I read.'

'In the van, sir. I met Wardle at Calvert's Corner kiosk. I left my own car and we did the company visit in the van.'

'The meeting was arranged – the meeting between you and Wardle, I mean?'

'Yes, sir.'

'When? When was the arrangement made?'

'Boyle – Constable Boyle – telephoned Wardle. Told him to wait at the kiosk till I joined him.'

'Boyle?'

'Constable Boyle. He was on office reserve duty that night.'

'He telephoned Wardle?'

'Yes, sir.'

'On your instructions?'

'Yes, sir.'

'Boyle will bear that out?'

'Yes, sir. He'll . . .' He cleared his throat, then continued, 'He'll have it logged in and logged out. Should have.'

'Logged?'

'The Telephone Log Book. All incoming and outgoing calls. To keep a check. It's – er . . .'

89

'Yes?'

'Sometimes they don't. That's all. They *should*. That's the system. But if they think it's an unimportant call – not worth logging – sometimes they don't.'

'They?'

'Whoever's on Office Reserve Duty – switchboard duty. They aren't all one hundred per cent reliable.'

'And this time? The time we're talking about? What if this Boyle character wasn't, as you put it, "reliable"?'

'I don't know, sir. I didn't check. I should have . . . but I didn't.'

'You should have.' I nodded short agreement, then rubbed salt into the small wound by musing, 'The situation – as I see it. It's around midnight. You're out checking the patrolling constables in the section. You decide to visit Gauntley. You know Wardle is at this telephone kiosk. You ring the office – this office – and tell Boyle to contact Wardle at Calvert's Corner kiosk, and tell him to wait there until you join him. Right, so far?'

'Yes, sir.'

'Fine.' I watched his eyes, saw them shift a little, then asked, 'Which kiosk?'

'Sir?'

'You telephoned the office from a kiosk . . . *which* kiosk?'

'The – er – the one . . .' He paused to think.

'Yes?'

'The one by the Carlton Bingo Hall – what used to be the Carlton Cinema.'

Beyond his right shoulder I could see Moody, and Moody was shaking his head, very slowly.

'Sure?' I asked.

'Well – er . . . yes. I – y'know – I think so. It's a long time since.'

'Eleven weeks . . . thereabouts.'

'Yes, sir. That's what I mean. A night's patrol duty. They all merge into—'

'The hell they do!' I snapped. 'Not this one. This one had murder attached to its tail. This is one night's patrol duty you'll *never* forget.'

90

Ask around. Ask men and women who interrogate for a living. Working jacks. Barristers. Solicitors. Investigative journalists. They'll tell you. The point arrives when you know you're hitting buttons. When you know the kewpie doll prize is yours for the taking. When you *know*.

Like now, but *not* like now. I also knew men and that, too, is important. With some a good push at this moment might have burst the dam. They would have tumbled and, whatever the truth was, it would have been mine within minutes.

But with this one . . . no way.

This one was just opening his mouth and letting anything come out. *Anything.* Maybe it was the truth. Maybe it was one long squirt of crap. Maybe a mix of both. Maybe he really couldn't itemise everything that had happened on the night of the thirty-first. Maybe just about any damn combination of anything and everything.

The guy was scared witless. He was talking, because some crazy logic insisted that he had to keep talking. Had to come up with answers, even if they were non-answers.

I'd met the sort before; to them personal disagreement equated with guilt. Not to be able to say something meant you'd something to hide. Stop answering questions, and nobody was ever going to believe you again.

I grinned at him. I tried hard not to make it the grin of a tiger ready to pounce. I had the impression that the grin frightened the daylights out of him.

I settled back in the chair, and said, 'Relax, Sergeant.'

'S-sir?'

'Coffee time.'

'I – I'm sorry, sir, but—'

'Or tea, if you prefer tea.' I looked at Moody and said, 'Do the honours, Sergeant. Mine's coffee. Three cups, and biscuits if you can find any.'

Moody straightened from his chair. He either knew the gag, or guessed there was a gag attached. He left his clipboard and pen on the seat of the chair, then vacated the room.

I took my time. I made believe that this was 'interval

91

time' and fished cigarettes and a lighter from my pocket. I enjoyed a couple of tenative draws on the cigarette before I spoke again.

'Pleasant place,' I observed quietly. 'Easedale. First time I've been here. I rather like it. It must be pleasant policing here.'

'It's . . . nice.'

He was having difficulty in making up his mind. Was I *really* letting him off the imaginary hook he figured himself to be on?

'Damn!' I made a tiny chopping movement with my hand. 'We didn't decide. Tea or coffee. You didn't say which.'

'Er – tea.' He tried to smile. He even tried to make it a pleasant smile. He took a deep breath, then said, 'Sergeant Moody knows. I prefer tea.'

'Good.' I drew on the cigarette again. I glanced around, then said, 'A nice room.'

'Er – yes, sir.'

'Comfortable.'

'Oh, yes.'

'You wouldn't think you were in a police station.'

He let that observation go past without comment.

'Relax, Sergeant,' I urged. I pushed the packet a fraction of an inch closer to him across the desk top. 'Have a cigarette.'

'No, I . . .' His lips twitched in a quick parody of a smile. 'I don't smoke, sir.'

I pushed myself upright and strolled across the room to the fireplace. I stood with my back to the electric fire, feet astraddle and one hand in my pocket. The object was to look and sound matey. Everybody's favourite buddy and nobody's enemy. I admit to the difficulty – to the near-impossibility – but I tried very hard.

I said, 'Married?'

'Eh?' He looked quite startled.

'Married,' I repeated. 'Are you married?'

'Oh, yes. Yes, sir.'

'Children?'

92

'Three. Three girls.'

'A worry,' I suggested amiably. 'These days. I'd hate to be the father of girls.'

'Why?' And now, in a mild sort of way, he was fighting back.

'Morals,' I said airily. 'There aren't many twenty-year-old virgins about these days.'

'You think not?'

'A personal opinion.' I made believe I was backing off a little.

'A wrong opinion.'

'Oh!'

'They aren't all like . . .' Then he suddenly closed his mouth and stopped talking.

There was a period of non-conversation. It was, of course, a silence, but it was in no way an awkward silence. Indeed, as it stretched out, it even took on a certain warmth. Very gradually, the interviewer/interviewee relationship melted away. We became, instead, fellow-coppers.

Nor had we spoken again when Moody arrived back with a tray holding two coffees, a tea and a plate of digestive biscuits.

Moody passed the refreshment round and the comfortable silence continued as we sipped and crunched.

The tap on the door was no warning; the knob turned and the door was flung open at the same time. A uniformed constable blurted his message to Poole before I could swallow biscuit crumbs and voice my disapproval.

'Sergeant. Alex Wardle's killed himself. His daughter's just telephoned.'

IX

Actually he hadn't, but he'd had a damn good try.

I should have known it – the uniform should have given me a clue – Poole was on duty. He'd been on duty since mid-morning, and the spell in the Interview Room had merely meant that the Easedale coppers had known exactly where to get at him.

In fairness, Poole had moved into action with surprising swiftness. Maybe he'd been very glad to remove his backside from the inquisitorial chair.

He'd murmured, 'Excuse me, sir,' as he'd hurried from the room, and I'd been left there, holding a cup of coffee and still munching biscuit.

I had shown great presence of mind – an amazing degree of self-control – and instead of bawling somebody out, I'd sipped coffee, looked at Moody and murmured, 'Policing! It gets more like a French farce by the day.'

'Sir?' Moody had still been flabbergasted.

'People,' I'd explained. 'Doors. Various members of the cast dashing in, dashing out, generally making idiots of themselves. Any minute now, some hairy-arsed constable will open the door and stagger in with his trousers round his ankles.'

X

Wardle had not succeeded in killing himself, and for that I was duly thankful. It would have made a most untidy ending to the enquiry. He'd taken dope – sodium amytal capsules he'd been prescribed for insomnia – a moderately large overdose, followed by half a tumbler of neat whisky.

He undoubtedly would have killed himself – it had been no mere 'gesture' – but his daughter had come home earlier than expected and had telephoned for an ambulance. Even then it had been a near thing; an emergency plumbing job with a stomach pump.

Poole telephoned from the hospital, to let me know, and at the same time apologise for his swift departure from the Interview Room. And the man who brought the news of Wardle's almost-resurrection was a character called Boyle – Police Constable Boyle – and (according to Moody) Police Constable Boyle had been on duty in Easedale Police Station on the night of the Wardle killing.

'Is that right?' I asked.

And Boyle bobbed his head and said, 'Oh, yes sir. I was Office Reserve. It was a very busy night, sir. A *very* busy night.'

'Which beat are you working at the moment?'

'No beat, sir. Office Reserve again. Till ten o'clock. They seem to like me being Office Reserve.'

'They?'

'The sergeants. The two section sergeants. When they make out the duty rota, they very often put me on Office Reserve.'

'Fix things.' I turned to Moody. 'If we can't have Poole, we'll have Boyle. Get somebody to take over. Then get back here.'

As he left the Interview Room, I added, 'Any awkwardness, any hesitation, throw Needham's authority around.'

Moody left. I guided Boyle to the chair recently vacated by Poole. I returned to the chair I'd been sitting in, and we awaited the return of Moody.

A word about Office Reserve Duty. Sometimes – and especially during the day – it is one of those jobs performed by civilians. It entails receiving telephone messages, logging those telephone messages. It needs patience, but little intelligence. As far as uniformed constables are concerned, it is a duty usually reserved for the numbskulls whose handwriting is at least legible. Often, it is a means of removing a particularly useless constable from the streets. Occasionally it is used as a form of mild punishment for stupidity, or over-enthusiasm, not quite deserving of a disciplinary charge.

Boyle, it would seem, was regularly on Office Reserve Duty.

We sat in silence. Without making it obvious, I checked on Boyle's reaction to silence . . . to the waiting for the unknown. He was either dumb or remarkably stoical. Accepting that he might have little, or even nothing, to worry about, the fact remained that he must have known my reason for wanting to ask him questions, and he

95

certainly knew the great chasm in rank between us. Nor, on the surface, was he one of the nonchalant types. Which, by my reckoning, made him dumb.

Moody returned, took up his position again, fed a clean sheet into the clipboard then glanced at me, indicating that he was ready.

'The night the Wardle body was found,' I began. 'You were on duty here at Easedale Police Station?'

'Oh, yes sir.' He sounded strangely eager.

'As Office Reserve?'

'All night, sir.'

'Right.' I settled down to the interrogation. 'Without checking with the Telephone Log – let's take things generally, rather than handling specifics at the moment – tell me what you remember.'

'It was Headquarters Radio Room that informed me. They telephoned. Poole had radioed in from Gauntley. I think he'd used Wardle's van. He wanted help, see? Mantell. He wanted Mantell at the scene. Oh, yes, and an ambulance. And general assistance.'

'Murder?'

'I wasn't told it was murder. Not at that time. I got the message from Headquarters, but nobody said it was murder . . . not at first. Just that things were urgent. That it was a major incident.'

'And that would be . . . what time?'

'Oh, after midnight. A couple of hours after midnight. Maybe more.'

'And that was all?'

'Later on – more than an hour later – Divisional Headquarters telephoned. I had to get Sergeant Backhouse out on duty, to take over from Sergeant Poole.'

'Backhouse?'

'He's the other section sergeant. Poole and Backhouse. They run the section . . . y'know. The usual thing.'

'The "usual thing",' I murmured. Then, 'Go on. What else?'

'Well, that was it, really. Backhouse told me about the murder. Somebody must have told him. Maybe Divisional

96

Headquarters. I suppose *they* knew.'

'Would they?' I asked.

'What?'

'Tell him. Tell this Sergeant Backhouse. *You* pulled him on duty on instructions from Divisional Headquarters . . . so why should *they* ring him?'

'There was a flap on,' said Boyle bluntly.

'Understandable.'

'Not telling people they should have told. Telling people they needn't have told. A complete cock-up. That's the truth of it.'

'Quite. But—'

'They didn't even tell Launder till Hunt had almost killed himself. Then it was just that Hunt had had the shunt . . . not about Wardle's missus being killed. He found that out when he came on duty.'

'Launder?' I asked.

'The super. Superintendent Launder. Nobody got round to telling *him*. They didn't even tell Wardle's daughter that her mother had been murdered. That her dad was in hospital. Not until somebody remembered . . . hours after it happened.'

'As you say, a cock-up,' I said gently.

Boyle bobbed his head in quick agreement and said, 'I think Eccles tried to keep things more or less under control.'

'Eccles?' I pretended ignorance more than was strictly true.

'Detective Inspector Eccles.'

'Oh!'

'I think he stayed at the scene most of the time.'

'Organising things?'

'I reckon.'

I stayed silent and waited for this Boyle character to keep talking. I knew he would . . . and he did.

He said, 'Hunt held a briefing in the back room. That was a bit later. When things had started moving. After six o'clock. I know it was after six o'clock. I should have been off, but I had to stay on.'

'A briefing?' I encouraged.

'The initial enquiry team. Back there, in the big room. I was still in the front office. Handling callers, and that.'

'Callers?'

'Yes. It was – y'know – getting out. About Wardle's wife. The media people. They wanted details.'

'Did they?'

'I didn't give them any. But they tried. I mean—'

'According to what you've said so far,' I interrupted. 'You couldn't give them any details. You didn't know any.'

'Ah, but—'

'Sergeant.' I glanced at Moody. 'Were you present at this briefing he's talking about?'

'No, sir.' Moody looked up from his foolscap. 'I was still at Hangman's Lane. I was there till lunchtime.'

'And you, Constable Boyle?' I eyed Boyle for a moment, then said, 'I have a rank.'

'I – er – I don't—'

'So has Superintendent Launder. So has Detective Inspector Eccles. You could even surprise us all by slipping a "sir" in occasionally.'

XI

Needham was turning out to be quite a character. He'd sent word out to Easedale that he was dining at the Thatched Oak; that he'd booked a table for two, and that he'd like me to join him for the meal. And why not? If he wanted a first 'progress report', that was his privilege. But I was wrong. He didn't want a 'progress report', he merely wanted to talk about the Wardle killing and, maybe, sketch in more details of the pros and cons of what had been a remarkably slap-happy enquiry.

'Like a ship without a rudder,' he said.

We were ordering. We were in the lounge, quaffing beer and lager and, as the waiter took our order and left for the kitchens, that is what Needham said.

'Like a ship without a rudder.'

'It must have knocked things a little off course,' I remarked.

'They were never on course.'

'Oh!'

He tasted beer and said, 'Hunt is related to the chief. A cousin or something.'

I said, 'Oh!' again.

'The joys of nepotism,' he said sourly.

'Hence "detective chief superintendent".'

'Lyle.' He indulged in a heavy sigh. 'Why is it that some men – especially chief constables – think that policing is such a push-over?'

'Chief constables?' I raised an eyebrow.

'*Especially* chief constables. *Some* chief constables.'

'They're not working coppers,' I suggested.

'They're not coppers, period. They're admin wallahs. That's why they make top office. Not because they know much basic street-work. Nor much about feeling collars.'

'Maybe he thought this cousin – or something – knew a lot about feeling collars.'

'Hunt,' said Needham, 'was your average detective sergeant, with a big mouth and more rank than he could handle.'

'I've known some good detective sergeants.'

'So have I. But they didn't stay detective sergeants.'

That was one I didn't care to answer, so I stayed dumb and sipped lager.

Needham swigged from his glass, dabbed the moustache of froth from his upper lip with his handkerchief and glanced around the lounge; at the oak beams and the surfeit of horse brasses; at the log fire and the collection of muzzle-loaders racked up one of the walls.

Very quietly, very deliberately he opined, 'Mind you . . . only bastards make good coppers.'

'I wouldn't say that.' I gave him the benefit of the doubt, and decided he was indulging in some involved game of off-beat humour.

'I would.' The solemnity of his expression showed he wasn't joking. 'What other species rewards its fellows for

99

tracking down and incarcerating its own kind?'

'The rogues of the species,' I reminded him.

'Rogues against rogues,' he insisted.

'I can't agree.' Maybe the man was playing Devil's advocate, maybe he was trying to push me into some sort of a corner . . . maybe anything. It was a ridiculous proposition, and I wouldn't wear it. I added, 'It's that, or mob rule.'

'And B.P?' he asked softly.

'Eh?'

'Before Peel? Before the various Town Police Acts, the County Police Acts . . . what then?'

'Hue and Cry. Watch and Ward. The Bow Street boys. The odds and ends Peel reorganised into a single police service.'

'Oh, come on, Lyle, you know better than that.'

'We take a lot for granted,' I conceded.

'We take street lighting for granted. We take a basic degree of safety for granted. Check the facts, Lyle. Even *after* Peel the murder rate was accepted as part of "normal life". In Ripper's London there were two, three, four killings a week. Almost as bad in rural communities. Footpads. Highwaymen.'

'Therefore?'

'Mob rule against mob rule, that's "therefore". And our "mob" is better organised. Better disciplined. Has better weapons. And in the final analysis has the biggest "mob" of all – the army – at its back, ready to smash all possible resistance.'

'As it should be, surely?'

'As it should be.' He nodded, but it was a slow, sad and almost a reluctant agreement. 'It's still the might-is-right argument, though. The individual gets hammered into the ground.'

'The "individual" villain. The "individual" murderer. Do you object to them being hammered?'

'Tell me.' The smile was friendly enough, but it carried a lot of cynical sadness. 'The murderers you've met. Bad men? Evil women?'

100

'Not necessarily. But—'

'They each committed the big crime,' he reminded me. 'Not too long ago any, or some, of them could have taken that walk to the hanging shed.'

'We've become more civilised. That's how the argument goes.'

'They're not *criminals*. That's what I'm getting at. Discount paid killers, contract men, those who commit murder in the course of violent crime . . . the rest aren't *criminals*.'

'What the hell are they?' I asked bluntly.

'Unfortunates,' he suggested. 'People with a low tolerance threshold. Men – women – who've been fed more than they can take. Who've cracked. Lashed out.' He paused, then continued, 'They're human, like the rest of us. Potential killers, like the rest of us. Like whoever killed Tabitha Wardle.'

I stared at him. I wished he hadn't said that, but having said it, I wanted him to say a lot more.

He drained his glass, put it down on the mat on the table, then wiped his mouth with the back of his hand.

'I'm not saying this,' he warned. 'This conversation hasn't taken place. That, I hope, is understood.'

'If that's what you want.'

'I don't just want it . . . I demand it.'

'Just tell me,' I said. 'I need to know.'

'That's why you're being told.' He smiled, then said, 'The woman, Tabitha Wardle, she was quite unique.'

'Not unique.' It was time I shocked him a little, too. I said, 'She wasn't the first nymphomaniac. She won't be the last.'

'You know?' He sounded surprised.

I growled, 'Short of sky-writing, everybody's gone out of their way to play nudge-nudge-wink-wink. She was cock-happy. Big deal! Some of them are. They still shouldn't be killed for it.'

'Not "cock-happy",' he said in a low voice. 'That's the trouble with this damned job. Blacks and whites, and what you don't understand, you don't believe.'

'That's about it,' I agreed.

'Nymphomania.' His voice was still low, and still very solemn. 'Ask around, Superintendent. Make enquiries. From people who know . . . not from idiots who scrawl dirty writings on lavatory walls. It's a real disease. A sexual disease. A *mental* disease.' A pause, then, 'It's a shameful disease . . . and very often, those who have it are, indeed, ashamed of the urges they can't control.'

'Uhuh.' I nodded, then finished my lager. The waiter was gliding towards us, presumably to let us know our table was ready. I growled, 'Like you say. This conversation hasn't taken place.'

XII

It had been a nice meal. It had been a *very* nice meal. The wine, too, very nice. And the cheese and biscuits. And the coffee and the brandy. Especially the brandy.

And now I was slightly rubbery – not too much, but enough not to give a damn – and I was moving in a not-quite-straight line down the path of the Thatched Oak garden, gulping good country air and trying not to act and think like the town drunk.

Nevertheless, it made a change, and a pleasant change. I couldn't remember when I'd last been tipsy but, I solemnly decided, I must make a point of doing it more often. There was a pleasant numbness, and an equally pleasant tendency to smile – even chuckle – for no good reason at all. But that was reason enough . . . to smile, to grin, to chuckle, to giggle for no better reason than that it was pleasant to do so.

I left the path and meandered across the grass. Like every idiot, I was attracted by the lights – especially moving lights – of the cars which were being driven from the car park. The large car park alongside the inn.

The slight slope of the grass down to the tarmac surface was giving me some difficulty. My feet seemed to be knitting themselves into an impossible knot. I fell forward, rolled down the grass and ended up on the edge of the tarmac. I was drunk enough not to be hurt, sober enough to feel a fool and drunk enough not to give a damn. I was also having some difficulty in hauling myself upright.

The voice said, 'Come on, sir. Let's get you back inside.'

I recognised the voice, but I must have been wrong. The owner of the voice had no business being at the Thatched Oak at that time in the late evening. I pushed the alcohol fumes aside long enough to check that I wasn't wrong. It was Moody.

Again it didn't matter a damn.

Somebody – Moody – helped me to my feet, then draped my left arm across his shoulders. Somebody else took my right arm, but this time the shoulders were not as broad and I felt the softness of feminine contours against my side. I smelled the hint of good perfume. I felt the touch of soft hair against the back of my hand.

A voice said, 'Come along, Superintendent. I think you should be in bed,' and it was a woman's voice. A young woman's voice.

By the this time I was not merely tipsy. I was stupidly drunk. I'd made a big mistake. In the dining room, when Needham had left for home, I'd been warmly fuddled. I'd figured that the evening air would clear my brain of the muzzy light-headedness. I'd been wrong. The 'good, country air' had mixed with the fumes and I'd finished up completely squiffed. Legless, in fact, literally.

We made our weaving, stumbling away across the grass and towards the entrance. Somewhere, not far from the door to the Thatched Oak, the female struggling with my right arm handed over to a stronger and more muscular person, and a man's voice said, 'Gently, sir. Gently. We'll soon have you inside. We'll soon have you safely tucked up in bed.' I recognised that voice, too. It was my reluctant friend, the waiter.

Thereafter, it was a straightforward head-and-tail job. Moody took my shoulders and the waiter tucked a leg under each arm, and that was it.

In a vague dozy sort of way, I was aware of being

103

carried, feet first, into the inn, along passages, into the lift, then along corridors and into my bedroom. It seemed quite a pleasant method of travel. I was dumped onto the bed. My shoes were removed, my tie was loosened and the duvet was thrown over me.

Thereafter, I slept.

XIII

There was no hangover. This surprised me. Maybe it was because fine food accompanied the booze. Maybe it was because the booze was of a certain standard. I know little of these things . . . only that there was no hangover.

I showered, shaved, changed clothes, then wandered down to the foyer. It was not yet quite dawn, but I was well refreshed, and the last thing I wanted to do was to return to my bed.

The night porter was seated behind the reception desk, reading a paperback. He put the book aside as I approached. I asked about first breakfast, and he told me 7.30 a.m.

'I can fix tea and toast for you now,' he offered.

'One slice,' I smiled. 'And honey?'

'Honey it shall be.'

'I'll take the morning air,' I said. 'How long d'you reckon?'

'Fifteen minutes. Maybe less.'

'Perfect. And – if you've no objections – here. With you. Better than a deserted dining room.'

'No objections at all,' he grinned.

The night porter disappeared into an office beyond the reception desk and I made my way into the greyness of a pre-dawn morning.

The tarmac shone with the dampness of the night. The grass was soaked. At a guess, the temperature was almost down to freezing. The whole world had that not-still-dark-but-not-yet-light quality known only to night workers, and easily familiar with foot patrol constables.

104

I liked it. I had always liked it. Three decades back, when I'd walked the pavements, it had been the one hour of the whole day which for me had had its own magic. Early shift railway men, newspaper delivery drivers – a very limited section of the working population – are on the streets at that hour.

A parallel: be about to decorate a particularly grubby room; be finished with all the pre-decoration preparation; open a new tin of good paint and have a new brush ready in your hand. There is a delightful feeling of expectation . . . equally at that time in the morning.

I walked alongside the grass down which I'd rolled the previous evening. I did a circuit of the deserted car park. I left the grounds and stood, for a moment, by one of the pillars of the entrance gates.

Take your choice. It was a dead world or it was a new-born world. Or, if you will, it was a still-born world. It was certainly something it would never be again . . . not until the earth had had one more complete spin.

I walked slowly back to the inn and arrived at the reception desk as if I'd timed it to the last split second.

I moved a high-backed chair from its position against the wall of the foyer and we used the desk top as a makeshift table. We chewed slightly burned toast and sipped cheap tea as we talked.

He asked the usual lead-in question.

'Are you getting anywhere, sir?'

'That,' I said carefully, 'is difficult to assess. I know some of the people better than I might have known them. Maybe better than they think I know them.'

'Is that it, then?' There was a twinkle in his eye as he asked the question.

'What?'

'Detection? Is that what it boils down to? Knowing people?'

'It helps.'

'What about clues?'

'After all this time? Fly-buttons in the flower bed?'

'Aye. I reckon.' He nodded understanding. 'Just people.

105

Just *knowing* them, eh?'

'Something like that.'

He chewed honeyed toast, sipped tea, swallowed then almost off-handedly said, 'I knew her.'

'Mrs Wardle?'

'I knew her,' he repeated. 'Nice enough lady. Pleasant. But too many folk made fancy excuses. That's my opinion.'

'Fancy excuses? For what?'

'Do I have to tell you?'

'You do now,' I assured him.

'She was a bit, y'know.'

'People made excuses,' I murmured.

'Aye.'

'Did she do anything that needed an excuse?'

'She liked men.'

'Did she?'

'Oh, aye.'

'Which means,' I said, 'she wasn't a man-hater.'

'You know what I mean.' He almost winked.

I joined him in the toast-chewing stakes, then said, 'I know what *I* mean. The truth is you're far too coy for me to know what *you* mean.'

'Sam Cooley . . . and others.'

'Now I *really* don't know.'

'Sam Cooley.'

'The name means nothing.'

'It meant something to her, you bet.'

'Tell me,' I said pleasantly, 'has anybody got around to explaining to you that you're a particularly prize specimen of a pillock?'

'Hey, look here. You can't—'

'I can. I will.' I smiled at him with my mouth, but not with my eyes. I spoke soft, reasonable-sounding words, but they weren't reasonable and gradually they scared the crap out of him. I said, 'I think you have a very cushy number here. At your age you don't need much sleep. You start . . . at what time?'

'Eight o'clock of an evening. Till six.'

'Ten hours. Most of it sitting here reading a book. Tea and snacks available. A reasonably good wage. Tips here and there. Paid to sit on your fanny and watch things. Watch too many things. Take note of too many things. And having noted them, passing the scandal around. The Wardle woman. This man Cooley. Telling tales. Y'know, I don't think the management would approve.'

'Hey, Superintendent, you wouldn't . . .'

'I might even enjoy doing it, old man. I might even enjoy doing it.'

'Oh!' The tendency to wink wasn't there anymore.

'On the other hand—' I paused, then said, 'I'd like to know as much as possible about Mrs Wardle – and about this Sam Cooley character – in the course of my enquiries. You understand?'

'Well, of course. But—'

'That wouldn't be scandal-mongering. That would be helping the police. Just as long as you didn't stray too far from the truth, that is. Follow?'

'Yes, sir. Yes, *sir.*'

'About Tabitha Wardle,' I said, pointedly. 'Everything you know about Tabitha Wardle, Sam Cooley, and anybody else who comes to mind.'

XIV

I had a late breakfast. I stayed with the night porter until he was relieved at six o'clock, then we moved into a quiet corner of the near-deserted dining room and continued our low-voiced conversation there. For a man his age, he'd used his eyes. Nor was there any fault with his memory. He told me about the antics of Tabitha Wardle; about her temporary amorists; about her visits to the Thatched Oak.

'Didn't her husband guess what was happening?'

'Not a chance. The only times he visited here was on a duty visit.'

'But she used this place as a trysting house?'

'Aye. I reckon. But bobby Wardle doesn't drink much.

He never fluffed.'
'He'd be – y'know – laughed at, wouldn't he?'
'You bet. Talk of the village. He never tumbled, though.
I reckon we felt sorry for him, really.'
'Go on, then. What else have you seen? Who else did she
tumble around with?'
It went on and on. Variations on the same basic theme.
If this Wardle female had other humping spots, over and
above the Thatched Oak, it followed that she'd been a
remarkably busy dame. It also followed that hubby had
been a remarkably dumb bastard.

Nine o'clock arrived, and he was still spewing out the
garbage. On the acceptable basis that what I was being told
was, perhaps, fifty per cent the wishful thinking of a dirty
mind, that still made Tabitha Wardle one of the great
whores of the universe.

I'd already had toast and honey. I ordered one slice of
grilled bacon and a small portion of scrambled egg. I also
ordered a bread roll, butter, lemon marmalade and black
coffee. I quietly ate my way through this light breakfast
while the night porter continued his saga of supposed
eroticism.

In truth, the man disgusted me. Having found a willing
listener, he held nothing back. He told what he had seen,
what he had heard, what he suspected and what he
imagined and, because of my reason for being there, I
listened.

Eventually he was empty of all substantiated tales and
his theories were becoming more and more improbable.
Moody walked into the dining room, and I called a halt to
the flow.

'That's enough, old man,' I growled. 'More than
enough.'

'You said—'

'And now I say "enough". If I need more, I'll come
again. Meanwhile be advised: keep your lips tightly zipped
. . . and forget I asked.'

He blinked and nodded. He hesitated, then pushed
himself upright and wandered away. He passed Moody on

the way out of the dining rooms and Moody glanced at him with open distaste.

Moody took over the chair vacated by the night porter. There was a spare cup and saucer on the table. There was coffee in the pot. I waved a hand before I spoke.

'Help yourself.' Then as he poured I said, 'I think I owe you an apology.'

'That's not necessary, sir.'

'You and the young lady who also helped.'

'My fiancée. Susan.'

'I was plastered, but I didn't realise how plastered.'

'Really, sir. We didn't mind at all.'

'Just tell her, eh? That I'm sorry.'

'I'll tell her,' he promised.

We drank coffee, then I said, 'The truth is, it's lucky you were around to pick me up.'

'We came to see you.' He grinned, a little shamefacedly. 'I – er – I wanted you to meet her. I'm rather proud. Then I spotted the assistant chief . . . so we had a meal instead.'

'Good.' I drained my cup. 'Have another meal as my guests tonight . . . if, that is, your fiancée is free.'

'She'll be free, sir. She's a farmer's daughter. From round here. She – er – helps around the house. Her old man doesn't believe in women going out to work.'

'Careful. You're talking about your future father-in-law.'

'A nice chap, but very old-fashioned.'

'Anyway.' I stood up. 'Dinner at eight here. Meanwhile . . . a character called Sam Cooley.'

XV

Samuel Cooley it would seem was a hard nut. How hard? GBH hard. Unlawful Wounding hard. So Moody assured me, as we made our way to his parked car.

'The boys tend to treat him with respect,' he assured me.

'How do the men treat him?' I growled.

'We're . . .' He stopped before he'd even started the sentence.

109

'Go on,' I encouraged him.

'It's not easy for me to say, sir.'

'Try.'

'I don't want to sound disloyal. That's what it boils down to.'

We'd reached the car. He unlocked the door, climbed in and leaned across to tip the latch on the front passenger-seat door. As I joined him, I tried to ease his mind a little.

I said, 'Remember, Sergeant. I'm not a member of this force. I'm here on loan for a specific purpose. Interviewing Cooley is part of that purpose. I want to know what he's like. I want to know if he's been allowed to run wild . . . and if so why?'

'Yes, sir, but—'

'But nothing. You're here to help me. You're here to fill in the gaps. Whatever you say – whatever opinions you express – will be treated with absolute confidence. Because I have no axe to grind I personally don't give a damn. Now . . .' I looked into his face from a distance of a mere couple of feet. 'Answer the question, please. Why hasn't this clown Cooley been stamped on, if he's as mad as he seems to be?'

'He's mad.' He turned the key in the ignition, engaged gear and eased the car towards the car park exit. In a voice which showed reluctance, he added, 'He's been allowed to go mad.'

'Why?'

'Sir, we have a good inspector in Mr Mantell. A good section sergeant in Poole.'

'But?'

'They aren't "chancers", sir. Neither of them. It's "the book" all the way. Eccles—'

'Eccles?'

'Detective Inspector Eccles. He'd have a go. I know he would, but he has an armful, what with all the other crimes in the division. He expects me to keep tabs on the Easedale crime. That means I come under Mantell . . . and under the eye of Poole.'

'And if you weren't?' I asked, with some curiosity.

As he eased the car into the stream of traffic, he said, 'I'd tame him.'

'You could?'

'Never doubt it, sir. Judo. Ju-jitsu. Unarmed combat. Straightforward dirty fighting. We have a club at Beechwood Brook. We teach self-defence. Until I met Susan, I was there twice a week. Instructing. Sometimes just helping out.'

I nodded silent agreement as he flipped the stick up the gears.

I said, 'I think we should interview Mr Cooley. I think we should give him a chance to answer the questions in a civilised manner. One chance. If he doesn't take it, I think we should demonstrate how very uncivilised we are. I think we should surprise him for once.'

He smiled. He almost chuckled. For the moment, I was his flavour of the month.

XVI

Cooley was one of those guys whose neck doesn't go in at the sides; it sprouts from the shoulders, then goes straight up at the same width as the distance between the ears. And the shoulders it sprouted from looked as if padding had been added under the skin. His hair sported a yard-brush trim and, to round everything off very neatly, it was a golden blond colour.

Way back – more years away than I care to contemplate – I'd served for a few years in the RAF. I'd seen PT instructors with those sorts of muscles and with that sort of hair.

I disliked the bastard on sight.

He led us into the living room of his once-upon-a-time farmhouse, then waved us into two deep armchairs.

He spoke to a female who watched us with rolling and cow-like eyes. He didn't mince his words.

'Blow, doll. Nobody wants you around when we're

talking business.'

She obediently 'blew', flopping her loose-fitting slippers on the polished oak floor as she went. She obviously knew her place and knew what she was . . . a slut and a door-mat.

As she closed the door, I said, 'Business?'

'Sure. What else?'

'Questions. We ask. You answer. We aren't selling, we aren't buying . . . we're interviewing.'

'What did you say your name was?' His eyes narrowed.

'Lyle. Detective Superintendent Lyle. But if you can't remember that, "sir" will do.'

'You're not from round here, Lyle.'

'Does that matter?'

'Just that—'

'Just that you knew Tabitha Wardle,' I interrupted. Then added, ' "Knew" in the Biblical sense.'

'Hey, what is this?' He was suddenly very suspicious.

'It's a murder enquiry, friend. It's a situation wherein we insist upon answers to some very hairy questions.'

'You're not from round here.' The observation was repeated with a degree of wonderment. It was almost a question. He snarled, 'If you *were* . . .' then left the sentence unfinished.

'What?'

'The tone's wrong, copper. Ask Moody here. I have a very short fuse. I don't like being talked to like this.'

'And who the hell cares what you like?'

'This is my bloody house.'

'Therefore be grateful,' I snapped. 'Any sauce from you, Cooley, and we'll say the rest in a police cell.'

The muscles of his jaw were knotted and his breathing was being forced from behind clenched teeth.

I pushed myself from the chair, stood opposite him, and said, 'That's as far as you go, Cooley. From here on you provide only answers.'

'Out of this house, copper.' The man was on the point of exploding. He ground out, 'Nobody – *nobody* – throws that brand of talk at my face. Out! Your bloody puppet here can be witness. I've asked you once. Just the once. That's as far

112

as I'm going. Now . . . out or I'll throw you out.'

I smiled. It was a deliberate red-rag-to-a-bull smile. I'd goaded him – again quite deliberately – and we were now at the crunch. I glanced at Moody and moved my head in a single, tiny nod. He interpreted the signal perfectly. He stood up from his chair and walked slowly to the door of the room. He turned the key in the lock, then leaned with his back to the panels.

'Tabitha Wardle,' I said gently.

'If you think—'

'You were humping her.'

'Lyle, I'm gonna—'

'Humping her,' I repeated. 'Unknown to her husband, of course.'

'Lyle, I'll tear your bloody—'

'Her husband's a copper, of course. You were cuckolding a copper, for Christ's sake.'

'No more, Lyle. I'll not stand here in my own house and take that sort of crap. I'll not—'

'You'll take it,' I barked. 'Like it or not, you'll take it. Cuckholding a copper. Dangerous. You're the enemy. You're why we're here. Why Wardle's here. Why the Police Service exists. You and your festering kind. You're one of the evil bastards . . . and you were crazy enough to cuckold a copper.'

It cracked him. It was meant to crack him. Men like Cooley are animals in their passions, in their appetites . . . in everything. Where other more civilised men simmer and keep their rising temper under check, the Cooleys of this world explode, go mad and – if the opposition has the situation under control – lose everything.

He came at me with his arms outstretched and his fingers curled, ready to grab. I side-stepped, put a wrist-lock on him, faced him towards the door and let his own momentum shunt him into a sprawling heap on the carpet.

Moody balanced himself on the balls of his feet and waited for Cooley to jump to his feet. Thereafter, it was not too far from a ballet of systematic, destructive violence.

113

Cooley swung a punch which, had it connected, would have ended Moody's contribution to the fracas. It didn't connect. Moody moved his head no more than a couple of inches, caught the fist as it passed, spun on his heel and delivered a particularly vicious version of the classic Irish whip throw. The flying Cooley landed on his back, with one foot smashing the front of a rather nice bureau which stood against one wall of the room.

Cooley licked his lips, crouched on all fours and gazed up at the Detective Sergeant. A child could have read his thoughts. It wasn't as easy as he'd first thought it was going to be. This time the coppers, too, were playing rough. The next option – the obvious option with a man like Cooley – was to play dirty.

The standard lamp was one of those heavy-based, solid oak affairs and it was about a yard beyond his grasp as he crouched. He was going for it – the move was so obvious it could have been stamped in illuminated scroll across his forehead – and equally I could see Moody watching for the first muscle-tense. Cooley made a dive and, inches before his fingers reached the lamp, Moody's toecap landed in Cooley's ribs and knocked the breath out of him.

Moody took a step nearer the fallen tearaway, stooped, grabbed a fistful of shirt-front and hauled Cooley into a more or less upright position.

Moody murmured, 'Y'know, bastard, I've been wanting to do this for years.'

Thereafter came the most systematic, cold-blooded hiding I've ever seen delivered. Ruthless, but scientific. Cooley was making tiny animal noises of surrender before Moody called a halt, yet there were no broken bones and no broken skin. No blood, but an immeasureable amount of raw pain. The guts, the crotch, over the kidneys; Moody seemed to know just where and just how hard to land them. And Cooley had no answer.

Cooley ended up on his hands and knees in front of the hearth, with his head hanging limply from drooping shoulders. The breath was rasping from the back of his throat. His short-cut hair was soaking with sweat and drops of moisture dripped from his chin and nose, onto the rug.

Moody wasn't even breathing heavily. He hoisted a buttock onto the arm of the chair he'd vacated and gave his victim a few seconds to fully recover his senses.

Then he said, 'Superintendent Lyle was asking you a question.'

'About Tabitha Wardle,' I reminded him.

'I was screwing her,' he managed to gasp. He made the effort and nodded his head. 'Me. Anybody. She was easy meat. Ask around.'

'I'm asking you,' I said.

'That's it then.' He raised his head and looked up at me. He panted, 'I don't know who you are, copper. Only that you'll regret this bloody day. I'll have that fancy rank off your shoulders. I'll—'

'Nothing,' I snapped.

'If you bloody well think—'

'We're not even here.'

'Eh?'

'Just that. If we leave here – if we nick you and take you with us – you've resisted arrest. If we decide not to nick you, we haven't been here.'

'What the hell d'you think—'

'I don't think. I *know*. Notebooks, people in authority. We can prove we've never been near this place. Prove it a damn sight more positively than you can ever prove we have.'

He gaped.

I smiled down at him and continued, 'Cooley, tell me. Why the hell do germs like you figure you've cornered the market in fancy alibis? How come you think we can't play silly buggers just as effectively?'

'I'll – I'll get you,' he whispered. 'Both of you.'

'Dream of it,' I said gently. 'Dream of it, but hope your dreams don't come true. If they do, they'll be nightmares.' I flicked a finger and said, 'Up on the chair, Cooley. Let's pick up from the point when you decided to be foolish.'

He pushed himself upright, then flopped into the

115

empty armchair. He was licked. The periodic wince showed that he also hurt. The eyes – the neat mix of hatred and fear – told their own tale. This one was a changed man. Dangerous, in that given the very ghost of a chance, he'd try to even things up. But never again would he count himself big enough – tough enough – to tangle with coppers on a physical level.

I said, 'You were cuckolding Wardle.'

'I've already told you—'

'Nothing! So far you've been too busy pretending some sort of indignation. You were cuckolding Wardle.'

'If you say so.'

'More than me "saying so". You were seen. We can push a witness in the box and prove it.'

'That arsehole the night porter at the Thatched Oak,' he mumbled.

I smiled at him, and waited.

'I'll kill the bastard.'

I continued to wait.

He spat, 'She didn't have to be asked twice. Take *that* from me.'

'It happened,' I insisted.

'Yeah.'

'More than once.'

'You want pictures? You want photographs?' His lips curled. 'Lyle, I think you're a dirty-minded sod. You like thinking about these things. You like—'

'And when she threatened to tell her husband?' I snarled. 'When she'd had enough of you? When it was possible – more than possible – that Constable Wardle would be gunning for you? What then?'

'Eh?'

'Kill her. Keep her quiet. Keep the law from treading on your coat-tails.'

'*Wardle?*'

'He could have nailed you.'

'Wardle? Do you *know* Wardle?'

'I haven't yet—'

'Wardle,' he mocked, 'wore the fancy uniform. He

116

wasn't even a pantomime bobby. Let me tell you, Lyle, Wardle wasn't – still isn't – capable of nailing a butterfly to its card. You want to *see* Wardle, copper. You want to *talk* to him. Then you'll know. Just how bloody stupid you sound saying that I'm scared of a prat like Wardle.'

XVII

'Is he?' I asked.

'What?'

'Scared of Wardle?'

'No.' Moody braked, then changed down at the halt sign. 'I can't imagine anybody being scared of Alex Wardle.'

'Cooley called him a prat.'

'Common decency equates with prattishness, that's the way Sam Cooley thinks.' Moody eased the car onto the main road. As he changed up again, he said, 'Alex Wardle is either an excellent copper, or a dead loss as a copper. It depends on your viewpoint.'

'He wouldn't have done what we've done?'

'Not in a thousand years. The right way . . . or not at all.'

I remained silent. We were tucked neatly behind a furniture removal van when Moody spoke again.

'I enjoyed it,' he observed, without taking his eyes from the rear of the furniture van. 'I enjoyed taming the sod. But, y'know, it could have repercussions.'

'No way,' I assured him.

'There was the woman—'

'No way,' I repeated. 'I wasn't bluffing. *We weren't there*. All the way to the top office. All the way to Needham. And as much weight as we need. It will need a lot more than Cooley and his woman to even dent our alibi.'

He pursed his lips in a silent whistle of amazement.

'It's why I'm here,' I growled. 'Fair means or foul. I don't have the machine normally geared to a murder enquiry. It's a ridiculously long time after the event. The original enquiry was a complete balls-up. I have to have

117

something going for me.'

He digested what I'd said, then asked, 'What about Cooley? *Is* his name on the card?'

'Cooley, men like Cooley . . . their name is on every card in the pack. Until we've eliminated them by standing the killer in a Crown Court dock, Cooley remains a "possibility".'

He nodded at the slope of the windscreen. Maybe he was getting an angle on policing he'd never come across before.

I allowed another half mile or so to slide under the wheels of the car, then said, 'Wardle.'

'Uhuh?' He frowned, not quite understanding.

'The Cullpepper place.'

'The Mark Cullpepper Hospital.'

'I think we should call.'

'Oh!'

'Unexpectedly. Creep up on him, as it were. I think it might be interesting. Illuminating.'

'They – er – they might not approve.'

'Who?'

'The medics.'

'They might not,' I agreed. 'But let's give them the chance.'

XVIII

It was a tiny local hospital; four main wards and a couple of side rooms; a poky little out-patients department; a small X-ray set-up and enough expertise to insert a few stitches and at a pinch set the lesser bones of the body. It was a nice place – a cosy place – and assuming whatever was wrong wasn't likely to kill, the sort of hospital capable of sorting out cuts, bruises and belly-aches without making everything into a big production job.

The medics were the local General Practitioners, working on a rota basis. The nursing staff numbered no more than two dozen. The whole place had a very family atmosphere.

As we walked gingerly across the highly polished floor of the entrance hall we met Doctor Harrison. Moody knew him, and introduced us.

'I'd like to have a few words with Wardle,' I said. 'He's your patient, I think. You're his GP.'

'You know why he's in here?' Harrison looked a little unsure. He added, 'You do realise he's a sick man?'

'I know why he's in here,' I said.

'He's a very disturbed man, Superintendent.'

'That,' I smiled, 'is why I'm asking.'

'Ah, yes.'

He was a youngish man. The vocational hogwash still gleamed in his eyes and kept the cynicism from his voice. One day he'd realise that to a lot of people he was a cheap way of getting dope, a means of having a small but steady income without the inconvenience of working, an excuse for claiming non-existent ailments whose symptoms have been learned off by heart. One day . . .

Meanwhile he muttered, 'He really mustn't be upset.'

'Of course not.'

'I'd stay here and go in with you, but I have a very urgent appointment.'

'We're both police officers,' I soothed. 'Sergeant Moody here. He knows you. He knows Constable Wardle. He'll keep things on the rails. Anyway . . .' I moved my shoulders. 'It's not that I want to interview Wardle. Just a few points that need clearing up. No more.'

'Yes. Of course.' He was smiling and nodding before he spoke. 'I'm sorry, Superintendent. It's just that . . .'

'I know. The welfare of your patient must come first.'

'Exactly.'

We shook hands, he left and Moody and I walked towards the side ward, and Police Constable Wardle.

'Was all that a con?' asked Moody in a low voice.

'You heard. A few points to be cleared up.' I paused, then added, 'One point, really . . . did he kill his wife?'

We located the side-ward we were looking for. We entered and as Moody exchanged gentle pleasantries with the occupant of the only bed, I closed the door very firmly and slid the tiny chintz curtains across the glass panel of the upper half. Then I joined Moody at the bedside and was introduced to the man Madge Wardle was quite sure had murdered her mother.

I motioned Moody to a chair alongside the bed, but I remained standing. I looked down at the patient and saw a pale-faced individual with weakness and indecision stamped large across his expression. His tousled hair was a dirty grey. His eyes were moist and red-rimmed. He obviously cried easily and cried a lot.

In a quiet, but not very sympathetic voice, I said, 'Okay . . . why?'

'Sir?' There was a croaking, whipped-dog quality in his tone.

'Why stuff yourself with sodium amytal? What good was *that* going to do?'

'Peace,' he whispered.

'Peace from what?'

'From you. From sleepless nights. From trying to live without Tabs.'

'It won't do, Wardle.' I shook my head.

'Sir?'

'Nearly two months. For that first week, maybe. It happens sometimes. Not often, but sometimes. But not this long, Wardle. You've grown accustomed. Not completely, but enough. Inside – deep down – you've already accepted a life without your wife. So, back we go to the original question. Why?'

'You,' he breathed.

'Me?'

'You're here to stir it all up again.'

'I am,' I agreed.

'I can't stand that. Not again.'

'I've read the papers,' I warned him. 'I've read the file.'

'Yes, sir.'

'You weren't interviewed. Not *interviewed*. You were too busy having a very convenient attack of the vapours. Then Chief Superintendent Hunt was knocked out of the case.'

'Yes, sir.'

'You were lucky.'

'Lucky?' His forehead creased with non-understanding.

'Nobody got round to asking you awkward questions,' I amplified.

He looked worried, but stayed silent.

'Hangman's Lane,' I said. 'Why Hangman's Lane?'

'I – er – it was Boothroyd.'

'Boothroyd?'

'Henry Boothroyd. Indecent Exposure. That's why, sir.'

'Henry Boothroyd? Who's Henry Boothroyd? And what the hell has *he* to do with Hangman's Lane?'

'I'd booked him. He'd been up at court that morning. Indecent Exposure. In Hangman's Lane.'

'Hangman's Lane?' I cocked an eyebrow of disbelief.

'Yes, sir.'

'Who the hell did he expose himself to? Sheep? Cows? Why on earth should women wander up and down a God-forsaken place like Hangman's Lane?'

'The WI, sir.'

'Eh?'

'Women's Institute, sir. The Mother's Union. Some of them – just women of the village – they go in for flower arranging. Some of them do a bit of sketching and water colours. Hangman's Lane . . . that's where they go. It's nice and quiet. Unspoiled.'

Moody added, 'It's a village, sir. They go in for unions, institutes, clubs. That sort of thing. More than in a town. You have to—'

'Leave it, Sergeant.' My tone was cold and annoyed. Moody had broken one of the cardinal rules of interviewing. Don't help the guy at the receiving end. I growled, 'Wardle should be able to come up with his own answers.'

'Yes, sir.' Moody blushed.

I switched my attention back to Wardle, and said, 'Indecent Exposure?'

'Yes, sir.'

'But why visit Hangman's Lane?'

'That's where it happened.'

121

'Am I getting the right picture?' I narrowed my eyes and stared at him. 'This – what-do-you-call-him?'

'Boothroyd. Henry Boothroyd.'

'This Henry Boothroyd flashes his chopper in Hangman's Lane. And this is important enough to need the scene to be visited by yourself and a uniformed sergeant? At midnight? After this Boothroyd freak has been convicted?'

'Er – yes, sir.'

'Why?'

Wardle moistened his lips.

'Kinky . . . wouldn't you say?'

'No, sir. It's – it's—'

'That's the only reason?'

'Sir?'

'The only reason you drove along Hangman's Lane?'

'Yes, sir. That's – that's all.'

'Not because you heard shots?'

'Shots?'

'A shotgun being fired?'

'No, sir. Why? Why should anybody be firing a shotgun at that hour?'

'Your wife was *killed*, Wardle.'

'Yes. I know, but . . .' He stopped, and left his mouth slightly open. Then he breathed, 'We didn't hear shots, sir. That's not why we drove along Hangman's Lane.'

I nodded, then allowed him time to regain some sort of composure.

Then I said, 'I won't accept the Boothroyd excuse. Not yet. But we'll leave that for a while. Let's talk about you.'

'Sir?'

'You,' I repeated. 'You and your wife. The murder of your wife. Let's talk about motive.'

'Sir, I don't know what—'

'Your daughter seems to think you had motive and to spare.'

'I – I – I . . .' He seemed to have difficulty in breathing.

'Take your time,' I soothed. 'Just what she said. What she hinted at. I don't necessarily believe her. I don't necessarily believe anybody.'

'Sir, why should I . . .' He stopped, moistened his lips, then said, 'Why should *I* kill Tabs?'

'You loved her,' I said flatly.

'But of course.'

'She loved you.'

'Of course she did. We were—'

'All that reciprocal love . . . and she was cross-screwing like crazy.'

It stopped him as if he'd hit a brick wall. This time he closed his mouth and kept the lips tightly pressed together.

'The talk of the village,' I said gently. 'The gossip for miles around. Your daughter knew. Your daughter was aware that just about everybody else knew. Now – surprise me – tell me you *didn't* know.'

'I knew.' It came out as little more than a whisper. He said, 'Of *course* I knew.'

From Moody came a barely audible, 'Holy cow!' but I wasn't interested in Moody.

I saw what I was almost prepared to accept as unsubstantiated truth in Wardle's pain-filled eyes; eyes bright with the shine of held-back tears; eyes that told of more hurt than any man should have to suffer.

I said, 'I have to ask questions.'

'I know.'

'I'm sorry.' I couldn't remember when I'd last apologised for doing my job, but this time I meant it. I muttered, 'It has to be done. It's why I'm here. And I've heard a lot of gossip.'

'It's not gossip.' His fingers clenched and unclenched on the coverlet as he breathed the words. 'I knew what was happening. We both knew. Madge and me. Madge said it was an illness. She kidded herself. Tried to convince Doctor Harrison that it was some sort of illness. It wasn't. Of course it wasn't. It was Tabs . . . that's all. She was made that way.'

'It's one hell of a motive,' I said softly.

'I know that, too.'

'Did you shoot her?'

123

'No. I couldn't have. I loved her, Superintendent.'

'*Loved?*' I think I stared with some degree of disbelief.

'Sir . . .' He flicked his tongue across dry lips. 'You have a child. You don't stop loving it because it's deaf. Because it suddenly goes blind. Because it's spastic. You don't turn it off like a tap – the love, the affection – you don't not love it because of something that's not it's fault. For any reason. You don't stop loving it.

'With Tabs. Just the same. That side – the physical side . . . it's not *so* important. Books. The newspapers. The tabloids. They make a big thing, but it isn't. Not really. Nobody can build on that. Not on that. So it didn't really matter. She'd given me Madge. And I still loved her.' He gave a tiny, involuntary shudder. As if something cold and distasteful had touched his skin. In a slightly stronger voice, he said, 'It doesn't matter now, does it?'

'Doesn't it?'

'Not to me.'

'Wardle, I'd like to—'

'It matters to Madge. It gives *her* peace.'

'The overdose?' I asked.

'To kill myself. The talk would have been that I'd killed myself because I'd murdered Tabs. Madge would have believed it. Everybody. The pressure would have eased. It might still ease. Madge might be able to get back on course. Be herself. Start enjoying life again.'

'Does *she* know?'

'No . . . of course not.'

'It's hard to believe,' I said softly. 'The reasons, the cock-eyed reasons . . . they're very hard to believe.'

'Does it matter?' The question was asked in a low but very steady voice. 'Does it matter who believes what? I know what the truth is. And now . . . so do you.'

XIX

Did I believe him? That was the big question, and it was a question only I could answer.

The gut reaction was . . . sure I believed him. Nobody would pull a gag as outrageous as that in an attempt to wool-blind an even reasonably sensible man. 'I didn't kill her, because she was ramming away like crazy, and I didn't mind if that made her happy. That's how much I loved her.' That was Wardle's answer, and it was such an outrageous answer it couldn't possibly be an attempted con.

Unless, of course, it was a very involved con. A con so devious as to be bordering upon the crazy.

Moody drove with his usual care, and without interrupting my thoughts. It was lunch time – probably a little after lunch time – and at a guess he was contemplating a snack to keep his digestive juices working for the rest of the afternoon.

I said, 'Cafés, restaurants. Anything reasonably decent in Easedale?'

'As long as you aren't too ambitious.'

'Just a snack,' I said.

'The Wooden Spoon,' he suggested. 'It's just round the corner from the police station.'

'Fine.' I nodded. 'Make for there. Then before we eat, telephone Beechwood Brook. I'd like to see this detective inspector . . . what's his name?'

'Eccles.'

'I'd like to talk to him. He was there – in Hangman's Lane – pretty well all the time. Maybe he saw something he didn't mention in his statement. If he's available, fix things.'

'Will do.'

I hesitated long enough to decide whether or not to ask, then said, 'Wardle? Does his explanation make sense? To you, I mean?'

'Knowing the man . . .' His concentration upon the road ahead didn't waver, nevertheless the impression was that he was weighing every word very carefully. 'Knowing the man, I'm prepared to believe him. He's the sort of fool who would.'

'A fool?'

'Maybe that's putting it badly. He's foolish enough . . . that might be more accurate.'

125

'Foolish enough to kill himself . . . assuming he meant to kill himself.'

'I think we can make that assumption without much doubt.'

'Therefore, foolish enough to kill himself. Not merely to point the finger at his wife's murderer—'

'He wasn't going to do *that*.'

'—But, if anything, to accept the guilt of that murderer. To give what he calls "peace of mind" to his daughter: to give her that regardless of the cost to himself.'

'I've already said, sir. He's foolish.'

'He's more than that. He's stark, staring mad.'

'But honest.'

It was one hell of a decision to reach and yet, at that moment, it seemed to be the only decision available. I was old enough – experienced enough – to know that the workings of the human mind while under stress are quite unpredictable. Logic and reasonableness are both thrown aside. What in calmer circumstances would be recognised as minor lunacy takes on the status of clear and uncluttered thought. Suicide – even murder – becomes a sensible option. Strangely – illogically – suicide and murder are both somehow separated from the final consequences of both . . . death.

I mulled all this over, as we threaded our way through the streets of Easedale and finally parked in front of one of those find-one-in-every-high-street Olde Worlde cafés, The Wooden Spoon.

Moody made a quick visit to the Easedale Police Station, in order to telephone Beechwood Brook Divisional Headquarters, then we had a tasty enough snack, in comparative silence, before leaving for yet one more question and answer session. This time with Detective Inspector Eccles.

XX

Beechwood Brook. A moderately busy market town; population climbing up to the twenty thousand mark; the headquarters of a police division, with a superintendent

(Launder) responsible for the law enforcement within a heady mix of rural and urban acreage. The usual thing. The usual sort of divisional headquarters police station. A structure of angles and glass. A box-like monstrosity sprouting from a low-walled area of tarmac. Or if you like a giant cigar box standing in the centre of a car park. Somewhere, some not very imaginative architect is perhaps receiving royalties on his basic design. All new police factories now have that same unappealing look.

Inside, too. Unlike the Easedale nick, the Beechwood Brook DHQ had space and to spare. Wide areas of polished parquet floors, unsullied by much furniture. Standard chairs whose skeleton framework seemed to be made up of black painted angle-iron. High ceilings and wide windows. A cold, featureless place which smelled of disinfectant and Mansion polish.

A cadet manned the public counter and, on the suggestion of Moody, he telephoned ahead and warned the DDI of our arrival. We climbed wide and shallow steps, traipsed along surgically clean corridors and eventually entered a very airy office and came face-to-face with Eccles.

I liked Eccles on sight.

It happens sometimes. Nor can that immediate rapport be either explained or mistaken. The handshake is firm and dry; it is neither limp and half-hearted nor taken to be an immediate test of hand and wrist muscle-power. He grinned a genuine welcome . . . and it *was* a grin, not a fixed and required smile. Having introduced ourselves to each other, he waved Moody and me to conveniently placed chairs and opened the conversation.

'It's good to see you, Superintendent. This damned case – the Tabitha Wardle killing – we've been farting around with it for far too long. I suspect we've blown dust into our own eyes. I for one would like to see it cleared up.'

'I've read the files,' I said. 'All the statements – including yours – but I'd like something else. I'd like to get the "feel" of what happened that night in August. I'd also like to hear what conclusions were reached . . . official and unofficial conclusions.'

127

'It was a complete hash-up,' said Eccles bluntly.

'Why? Why should it be? A straightforward blasting away of a life. Why the hash-up?'

'Fear,' said Eccles. 'Terror, if you like. A realisation on the part of some people that regardless of what had been done, Hunt would find fault by the yard. That – justifiably or not – he'd go bananas as soon as he arrived on the scene.'

'As bad as that?' I raised my eyebrows.

'Ask around,' suggested Eccles. 'Poole. Mantell. Even Wardle. They'd met him in the past. He'd tongue-lashed them for little or no reason. They were scared . . . and they couldn't think straight.'

'They wanted him to come a cropper?' I asked. Then added, 'Consciously or sub-consciously.'

'Possible.' Eccles nodded. 'Maybe more than just possible.'

'Okay.' I fished fags and a lighter from my pockets. I offered the cigarettes around as I continued, 'Give me a complete picture. That night, blow by blow, minute by minute . . . as far as *you're* concerned, Inspector, what exactly happened?'

'About four-fifteen,' said Eccles carefully. 'That's about when the phone rang. I was in bed. Headquarters telephoned. A message from Mantell – Inspector Mantell, he was at the scene. What had happened. That Sergeant Moody, here, had been informed and that I was requested to attend.'

'About four-fifteen?'

'Uhuh.' Eccles nodded. 'I had just about time to splash water on my face and climb into some clothes when the sergeant arrived. Then off and away. The streets and roads were clear. We made good time.'

'And when you got there? To Hangman's Lane?'

'She'd been medically certified as dead. Mantell had seen to that. Wardle had had a bad time. He was in hospital.' He frowned, then said, 'Come to think of it . . . that was the first time I learned that it was Wardle's wife. Till then, as far as I was concerned, nobody had put a name to the body.'

'And then?'

'Then – let me see – oh yes, I detailed Sergeant Poole as coroner's officer.'

'Coroner's officer?'

'In effect.' Eccles grinned. 'We don't run to such alien creatures in this force, Superintendent. Very make-do-and-mend. The guy who finds the body gets the prize. But of course that was Wardle and he wasn't available. I lumbered Poole with the job. Stay with the corpse. Attend the post-mortem. Identify the body taken over by the coroner as the body found in Hangman's Lane. The normal three-ring circus.'

'And?'

'He – Poole – stood by the body. Him and a motor patrol man. Nobody else allowed in the field. Eventually, he accompanied the body to the morgue.'

'Fine.' I nodded approval. 'Good police procedure. Meanwhile, what about Mantell?'

'Mantell came back to Beechwood Brook. Arranged for Backhouse to take over from Poole at Easedale. Then started trawling for odd bods throughout the division for general footwork come first light.'

'And Chief Superintendent Hunt?'

'I notified him at about the same time. I telephoned him at his home from the kiosk at Calvert's Corner. That's in Gauntley.'

'I know.' I drew on my cigarette, then asked, 'Why phone? Why not use the radio link via headquarters?'

'Confidentiality.' Eccles didn't hesitate. 'Straight through, from phone to phone. Using the air waves . . . that would mean at least one cut-in – at least one officer I didn't know, and who might not be as reliable as I'd have liked.'

That was how he told the story. Simply, and without any exaggeration. He was, I decided, the sort of copper I liked. He was no headline chaser, but he was prepared to accept the responsibility of his rank . . . and perhaps more. He told of an episode with a marauding fox without excuse, but also without apology.

'And that was it?' I asked. I squashed my cigarette into

129

the desk ash-tray, continued my forward-leaning movement and stood up. As I walked towards the window, I said, 'Dawn. Had it reached dawn by this time?'

'Not far off.' Eccles chuckled, then added, 'The business with Logan happened before dawn.'

'Logan?'

'One of the scribblers from the local scandal rag.'

'Tell me,' I suggested.

He told me. He had a half-smile on his face during the telling. It was a typical piece of police arm-chancing . . . but dangerous.

Moody chipped in with, 'We had him worried. It's what he deserved.'

Eccles said, 'We took a chancer and it came off.'

'Both of you.' I gazed from the window. I saw roofs, damp with a slight drizzle that had started since we entered the DHQ building. I said, 'You were bored. Maybe a bit cold.'

'Could be,' agreed Eccles. 'I for one wanted some action.'

'A bloody stupid risk,' I opined. 'For no real reason and at the start of a murder inquiry. Little wonder everything went arse-over-tit.'

'Accepted,' said Eccles softly.

'I'm not from this force,' I reminded him. 'It has little to do with me . . . but it was still a crazy move.'

Eccles said, 'We got away with it. There won't be a next time.'

I passed the fags around again, then asked, 'Boothroyd? The name's been mentioned.'

'A flasher,' continued Moody. 'Wardle had had him in court that day . . . the day before the murder.'

'And?' Eccles looked puzzled.

'There's been a suggestion, a hint . . .' I spread my hands. 'Some of these perverted bastards. Who knows? Tit for tat. Kill the copper's wife.'

'A *flasher*?' Eccles's expression turned from one of puzzlement to one of incredulity. 'For God's sake, sir. Since when did a twisted little raincoat-opener—'

'I know.' I waved him silent. 'A silly suggestion, but it was made. And seriously.'

Moody said, 'He wouldn't have the guts.'

'That for sure.'

'Okay.' I drew on the cigarette. 'So that's it, until dawn.'

'That's it,' agreed Eccles. 'Suchet arrived and—'

'Suchet?'

'Inspector Suchet. Scene of Crime Officer. He came out with Hunt from headquarters. He'd dropped Hunt off at Easedale – for some sort of briefing. Suchet had brought some rolls of Scene-of-Crime tapes. Him and Moody, here, draped them around. Suchet dealt with the scene itself – the field. Moody used them to cordon off the whole of Hangman's Lane. And that was it. We settled down to wait for Hunt.' He smiled and said, 'A little worried, if the truth be told. He was a most irrational man. For sure, we hadn't done things "right". Not *his* way. When he arrived there was going to be a Brock's fireworks display . . . and nobody was looking forward to it.'

'Not a popular man,' I murmured.

'Not really,' agreed Eccles.

And that was it. We stayed there another hour, thereabouts, and the usual minor hospitality of tea and biscuits was provided. But nothing extra was added. I ended up with a better feel of the night in question. I learned odd little things about the way those at the scene had behaved; Mantell's old-maidishness; Poole's basic fear of taking chances; Suchet's peculiar effeteness coupled with a strange insolence. They were coppers. Various ranks. Different ages. But open any box – drive around any division – you'll come across their kind. Coppers are not all butch or barrel-chested. They aren't all thick. They aren't all polite, they aren't all sombre. They're like the rest of mankind . . . good, bad, indifferent, and sometimes pillocks.

That's what I learned, and I was grateful.

XXI

Moody tore the page from his notebook, and held it towards me.

131

He said, 'That's it, sir. That's what I mean. I tried to attract your attention when you were interviewing him. I couldn't. But he's either mistaken or he's lying.'

The page showed a roughly drawn outline-map of Easedale. The shape was a fat and flattened 'L', with the distances to Beechwood Brook and Gauntley shown. Two crosses showed the rough situation of a telephone kiosk and Easedale Section Station.

I frowned at the sketch for a few moments of silence.

We'd left the constabulary headquarters and we were part way between Beechwood Brook and Easedale.

Moody had pulled the car into a lay-by, then he'd muttered something I hadn't caught at first utterance.

He'd repeated, 'There's something you should know, Superintendent.'

'What's that?'

'Let me draw you a map, sir. It might explain things better.'

As he sketched the map and included the points of reference, he explained things.

'That's Easedale, okay? That's the way to Beechwood Brook. On this road. That's the way to Gauntley. That's the telephone kiosk – the one outside the Carlton Bingo Hall – the one Poole said he used to telephone Easedale police station, to tell Constable Boyle to notify Wardle to wait at the Gauntley kiosk. Get it?'

'I – er—'

'Sir, he'd have to pass the police station on his way to Gauntley. If he was at the Carlton Bingo place, why telephone? Why not just call in?'

He passed the torn-out page to me, and said, 'That's it, sir. That's what I mean. I tried to attract your attention when you were interviewing him. I couldn't. But he's either mistaken, or he's lying.'

'Lying?'

'Or mistaken.'

'Why should he lie?'

'He's – er – probably mistaken.'

'Mistaken? On that night of all nights? It's a little like not remembering where you were when Kennedy was assassinated.'

'Yes, sir. But . . .'

'I know, Sergeant. One of those snags. Maybe it was a mistake . . . but one of *those* sort of mistakes. Eh?'

He muttered, 'Yes, sir,' and he sounded miserable. It was the brand of misery visited upon Judas.

XXII

Moody dropped me off at the Thatched Oak, then left to spruce himself up for the dinner engagement. I strolled through the entrance foyer of the inn, and from the door leading to the lounge came a man who at second glance I recognised as Charlie Calverley. Charlie Calverley, the 'boom-boom' merchant. The front-of-the-curtain comic who'd once been capable of making an audience ache with prolonged laughter. Who'd once been able to out-crack any heckler stupid enough to take him on.

He looked considerably older than I'd expected, even without the disguise of stage make-up. Nevertheless, the bulbous nose was there, as was the Mephistophelian eyebrows. But the face lines were there, deep and harsh, and the hair was a dirty grey and wispy.

As he reached me, he held out a hand and said, 'You're the strange copper, right? Name of Lime?'

'Lyle,' I corrected him.

'I'm Calverley. Charlie Calverley.'

'I know.' As we shook hands, I added, 'A remarkably fine comedian.'

'Thanks.' He gave me a quick nod, as if in full agreement, then said, 'Can we talk? In the lounge, perhaps?'

'Why not?'

And in the lounge we shared a three-seater sofa – deep and luxurious – and it felt strangely like a separate room, not part of the lounge. A very private snug within an already deserted room. Calverley ordered two whiskies,

133

then as he sipped and chewed salted peanuts from a dish on a table within easy reach, he talked.

'You haven't been to see me.' It was almost an accusation.

'Should I have been?'

'Not much goes on around here that I don't know about.'

'That's what I've been told.'

'Therefore?' He lifted one of those once-famous eyebrows.

'Can you name the murderer of Tabitha Wardle?' I asked bluntly.

'Not that,' he admitted.

'That's the only answer I'm interested in. The only question I'm here to ask.'

'I can tell you who didn't.' He tasted whisky, then added, 'Can't prove it, but that's not important. I know damn well who's capable and who isn't.'

'That must be a very handy gift,' I said sarcastically.

I'd recently left a man I'd liked on sight. Calverley wasn't the same by a few light years. Calverley was the sort of guy I *dis*liked on sight. I had the distinct impression that the feeling was mutual.

He rapped, 'I came along to help.'

'Good of you.'

'My profession.' He threw another nut into his open mouth. 'It's not just telling gags. There's more to it than that. A hell of a lot more to it than that.'

'I wouldn't know.'

'I would. I earned myself something of a fortune by knowing.'

'That I believe.'

'To know the audience, see?'

'Coppers don't "perform". With or without audiences.'

'London and the provinces. Glasgow, Leeds, Brum, Cardiff. They're all different. It's a craft. Knowing what they're like. Getting the "feel" of every audience. It's the difference between good and great.'

I nodded. Despite my immediate dislike of the man, I

was more than a little fascinated by his explanation of his art.

'There's nobody in this village capable of killing,' he said, bluntly.

'Oh, for Christ's sake!'

'I've met 'em, Lyle. You – coppers – you're not the only people who meet murderers. People capable of murder.'

I tasted my whisky and waited.

'Speciality acts.' His eyes narrowed. 'Knife throwers, balancing acts, contortionists . . . that sort of thing. The first-after-the-interval turns. Lots of *them*. They'd kill, given the chance to get away with it.'

'I wish it was as easy as that.'

'It is. Enough years of experience, and it *is*. You can tell. *I* can tell. It takes a lot of hatred – a lot of disappointment – to build up the capability. Those "bar turn" performers, though. They worked, see? What they did was a damned sight more difficult – often a damned sight more dangerous – than what the top of the bill did. Some long-haired, squealing pop idol who can't sing and knows sod-all about music . . . I mean, I ask you. The specialities worked for peanuts, and the prats who topped the bill made money and treated everybody like dirt. You take it from me, copper, I've seen murder in other men's eyes before now. Often. I've come to recognise it.'

'And that's what you base your assessment on?'

'Nobody from this village,' he insisted. 'Don't look in Gauntley. You won't find him here.'

I moved my shoulders. I'd met men like Charlie Calverley so many times in the past. Argument – even logic – was wasted on them. The only way was to let them spout their opinions. Let it go in, then let it come out, without allowing it to lodge too long in the brain.

To save unnecessary hassle, I steered the conversation towards Calverley's own craft.

I moistened my lips with the whisky, then said, 'Y'know, Calverley . . . God knows when you first made me laugh. I think it was at Blackpool Opera House. Long before I joined the force.'

'That,' said Calverley, 'makes me feel very old.'

'You knew your job.'

'Of course.'

'I dunno . . .' I rubbed the nape of my neck. 'I don't understand modern comedy.'

'Does anybody? Anybody who doesn't howl with laughter at what's written on lavatory walls?'

'It's not like it used to be,' I encouraged.

'Hear-hear to that.'

'Not like the old days.'

'Not funny any more. Not clever.'

I examined Calverley's face. He had wrinkled features; a leathery skin, the sort of skin associated with jockeys – the skin and the tired eyes. The outward appearance of those who ride horses for a living . . . and who lose far more often than they win.

He said, 'Tits, bums, farting and fornicating. Take those away and the modern comic – so called – couldn't raise a smile.'

'Not like the old days,' I repeated.

'I remember the old Moss Empire circuit,' mused Calverley. 'Will Hay. Harry Tate . . . I can even remember *him*. Jimmy James. I was second-string comedian in those days. I'd stand in the wings and learn. The timing of the gags . . . immaculate! Magical. The same old gags. The same old routine. It never varied. But there was always a full house. Dammit, they'd heard it all before – seen it all before – but they still rolled in the aisles. It was the timing, y'see. The craft. To milk a gag, but to know when it was running dry. Myself? I was always a front-of-the-tabs man. No feed. Just me and the audience. Sometimes it wasn't easy.'

'Not easy,' I agreed.

There were a few moments of silent remembrance. Those weary eyes stared into the past. To when he could work magic from the apron of a stage; to when he could dominate an audience – lift them up, dump them, insult them, caress them, laugh with them or laugh at them – to when he was monarch of a packed auditorium. And quite suddenly I knew. Today the village, Gauntley, was his auditorium, and those who lived in Gauntley were his audience. He claimed to know so much . . . because years ago he *had* known so much.

Softly he said, 'The stand-up stuff. Sometimes it's a damn sight harder than Shakespeare.'

'I never did like Shakespeare. Not over-much.' I raised the glass to my lips. 'I could never quite understand the stuff.'

'Olivier did it well.'

'I wouldn't know. I'm no blank verse enthusiast.'

'But he couldn't do stand-up stuff.'

'Shakespeare?'

'Olivier.' A quick smile touched his lips. 'He pulled his guts out in *The Entertainer*. I saw it four times. But, y'know, he *couldn't*. Some of the pros – some of the front-of-the-tabs men – could have played it. Some of Osborne's gags weren't bad. Just the delivery, see? The delivery and the timing. I watched it four times, and every time I was just that bit sad. Not bad . . . not bad at all. But poor old Olivier wasn't a comic. He just didn't know.'

XXIII

I had a good hour before I was due to return to the lounge and meet Moody and his fiancée before dinner. The bedroom had a cosy warmth due to day-long central heating; a very private warmth, like heated cotton wool. Stripping off was almost a sensuous pleasure. Soaking in the bath, neck-deep in hot, sweet-smelling suds was positively hedonistic. The towels were large, white and fluffy. The linen, the shirt and the socks were all freshly-laundered. I dressed slowly and felt good.

As I dressed – as I carefully threaded each button through its button-hole – I stood by the desk, flicked various pages of the file and checked and double-checked.

Did I know the murderer at that time?

Know? That is a big word. It has a finality which only a

137

fool would take on board without something more substantial than the vague leads, hints and probabilities I had to go on at that time. And yet in my own mind – in the absolute privacy of my own unspoken thoughts – I knew.

Which, of course, meant damn-all at the time. Every ranking copper knows somebody who has committed a serious crime and, quite often, that crime is either murder or manslaughter. That knowledge is useless, without proof. Without enough evidence to make a conviction stick.

I knotted my tie very carefully as I contemplated various possibilities. To trip the bastard up. To make the smart-arse con being pulled work for *my* benefit.

I padded around the bedroom in my stockinged feet. On an impulse, I unlocked the tiny drinks fridge and helped myself to a tiny bottle of whisky and an equally tiny bottle of soda water. Then I sat on the edge of the bed and hashed and re-hashed the few facts – presumptions, the few firm speculations – that had surfaced since my arrival in Gauntley.

Nothing firm. Nothing with which I could go to Needham and say, 'There's your killer. Scrape around. Ask enough questions of the right people. Give the forensic scientists enough slivers, threads and dust particles from the right places. Do these things. Persevere. Then one long, hard interview . . . and you *might* get a confession.' But this was real life. This was no 'body in the library' literary puzzle.

Tabitha Wardle had had the life blasted out of her miserable body. What had soaked into the grass in Hangman's Lane had not been tomato ketchup. It hadn't even been Kensington Gore.

For some time a certain despondency threatened to overwhelm me. My thoughts ran counter to that direction which both training and experience demanded. Just temporarily: it was all so damned stupid – did it matter? . . . the over-sexed bitch had deserved everything she'd collected . . . it was wrong to kill, but it was also wrong to take marriage vows and thereafter hawk mutton to anybody interested . . . therefore, why take misery and add even more misery? . . . why not let sleeping dogs slumber on? . . . why not allow the bloody thing to stay undetected? . . . why not leave Gauntley and its miserable, unimportant inhabitants alone? . . . let them live their own mushed-up, silly little lives in their own lunatic way. Get back to Rogate-on-Sands. Get back to the much less important hassle of the running battle with Crosbie. Let the killer go to the grave in the erroneous belief that even suspicion had been warded off.

I sat there for a long time. For far too long.

Then I tipped the drink down my throat, stood up from the bed and slowly and carefully finished dressing for the dinner date.

PART THREE
Lyle's Cunning

7.35 p.m.

As Lyle walked into the lounge of the Thatched Oak, Moody stood up from one of the deep, chintz-covered armchairs and approached the Detective Superintendent with outstretched hand. They shook hands as if they were long-standing friends who hadn't met each other for far too long – certainly not as if they'd been in each other's company throughout the earlier part of that day.

Moody led Lyle to the chair he'd just vacated, then gave a wave of introduction towards the girl sitting on the matching sofa.

'This is Susan, Susan Morley, my fiancée. Susan, this is Detective Superintendent Lyle.'

Lyle and the girl shook hands, then Lyle lowered himself into the matching armchair to the one being used by Moody and Moody hurried off to the bar.

It was the usual pleased-to-meet-you-but-I-doubt-if-we'll-meet-again situation. The girl was pleasant enough, and age gave Lyle the advantage of setting the pace, nevertheless the small talk was quite meaningless. Both talked, but said nothing. Both heard, but didn't listen. They merely contributed to the general hum of meaningless conversation which washed around the room.

Moody returned from the bar. He placed a whisky and soda on the table in front of Lyle, then shared out the three menu folders he was carrying tucked under his arm.

As he sat down, he said, 'Fifty-fifty, sir.'

'Eh?' Lyle looked up from the menu.

'The cost.' Moody flipped the printed menu lightly with a forefinger. 'We share the cost. Straight down the middle.'

'No, we don't.' Lyle's tone brooked no contradiction.

143

'Neither of us pay. This meal, sergeant, is being paid for by the Calfordshire County Constabulary. Don't let the size of the bill worry you.'

'Not bad.' Moody nodded his head in approval. 'If Accounts will wear it—'

'They'll wear it,' Lyle assured him. 'Leave that side of it to me.'

Moody smiled and returned to consulting the menu. He ran his finger down the list of dishes available, checked the prices then choose the most expensive. The girl, on the other hand, seemed to choose only what she knew she'd enjoy. Lyle's eyes glinted with secret amusement as he watched. He, himself, chose moderately, then when the food was agreed upon, motioned a waiter to the table and ordered the meal.

9.00 p.m.

The woman would become a shrew. That was the considered opinion of Lyle. He watched and noted as they ate and exchanged the normal convivialities of dinner conversation. Without apparently meaning to – probably without even knowing – she criticised Moody throughout the meal. He'd chosen a quail and had picked one of the tiny drumsticks from his plate in order to nibble the flesh from the bone.

'Darling. Please don't.'

'Eh?'

'Not here. Not in a public restaurant.'

'It's too fiddling for a knife and fork.'

'Not with your fingers, darling. Not here.'

And he'd moved his shoulders in a tiny gesture of habitual resignation and complied.

And when the waiter had lifted the bottle to re-fill Moody's glass.

'I shouldn't have any more to drink, darling.'

'Eh?'

'You'll be driving, remember.'

144

'Oh!'

Moody had covered his half-empty glass with his hand and shaken his head at the waiter.

These things and other equally tiny pointers – the very choice of her words – had to Lyle *been* pointers. Given time – given a wedding ring – she'd develop into a domineering wife. She'd love – perhaps love too much – but she'd also possess. Stifle. She would demand complete obedience . . . and not even be aware of the quiet insidiousness of her mannerisms.

Lyle knew enough about life to make such predictions with a moderate degree of accuracy. He'd seen it happen too many times in the past. But for the moment the girl exercised her right to quietly criticise and Moody obediently accepted that criticism as one aspect of her affection.

But it was a pleasant meal. The food was good and expertly prepared. The talk was empty, but mildly interesting. The room had that warm, relaxed atmosphere of a place dedicated to the unwinding of everyday tensions.

Then the manager of the Thatched Oak entered the dining room and made his soft-footed way to the table occupied by Lyle, Moody and the girl.

He bent forward, and with a fixed smile on his lips, he murmured, 'Can you come to the phone please, Superintendent?'

'The phone?' Lyle looked puzzled.

'I think it's important sir.'

'Any idea what it's—'

'A Detective Inspector Eccles, sir. He's anxious to speak to you. And he mentioned Detective Sergeant Moody.'

9.20 p.m.

The night porter's name was Hardy . . . Oliver Hardy, which in the circumstances made for the hint of sick humour. Eccles told Lyle the night porter's name as they

145

gazed into the electric torch-lit interior of the chicken hut. Not that it mattered too much what name the night porter had once carried. It was now prefixed with the words 'the late'. Hardy was as dead as a squashed nit. He sprawled on the wooden floor of the shed, with his head held at an angle by the perch and his jacket and trousers filthy with the muck of hen droppings.

Eccles held the torch steady and said, 'I'm told he loved his chickens. All Buff Orpingtons . . . so I'm told.'

'When?' asked Lyle flatly.

'Found at about eight,' said Eccles. 'Apparently he usually books in there for his night stint at around seven-thirty. He didn't answer the phone. One of the hotel dogsbodies was sent round. Found him. We were notified – just before eight – and I attended. The medic's examined him. Death at around six . . . so he thinks. Manual strangulation, and not much of a struggle.'

'And other information? Other, that is, than his personal choice in chickens?'

'He wasn't too popular.'

'That I can well believe.'

They turned and strolled slowly towards the row of cottages less than a hundred yards from the chicken run. Three of them – Lyle, Moody and Eccles – solemn-faced, but not too shocked. It was murder, but because of the method it was bloodless murder. And this – despite the slightly protruding eyes and the bluish face – did not seem as violent, nor as permanent, as a gun-blast job.

Very tentatively Eccles said, 'A serial murder, perhaps?'

'I think not. Not *serial*.'

Moody expressed his first opinion, 'A man – a woman. Out in the country – in a hen hut. Shotgun – strangulation. No common denominator . . . not that I can see.'

'Both at Gauntley,' suggested Eccles.

'That I buy,' said Lyle. 'A village the size of Gauntley. Two killings within a few weeks. There's either a connection or this is a remarkably unhealthy place.'

'But not a serial,' insisted Moody.

146

'A connection,' said Lyle. 'One leads to another. One leads from the other. I'd say a distinct connection.'

'But not—'

'But not a serial killing.'

The cottage was one of a row of four; railway cottages which had once flanked a tiny station, long ago when Gauntley could be reached by rail. There was what had once been a cobbled yard, with grass growing between the domes of the cobbles. There was even a slabbed slope which led to a point where the platform had started. The whole place had an odd and strangely creepy feel. As if the tattered remnants of the late 1920s had been caught in flight and pickled in aspic.

Lights were lit in all four cottages. Uniformed constables were stationed at strategic points around the houses and their surround. Two squad cars were parked on the grass-grown cobbles.

They entered the cottage – a low-ceilinged, basic living place – and gazed around the room where the dead man had once lived. All three men kept their hands firmly in their pockets.

'A dump,' observed Moody.

'But his home.' Lyle turned to the Detective Inspector and asked, 'Again . . . what was his name?'

'Hardy. Oliver Hardy. Widower. No family. He worked as night porter and odd-job-man at the Thatched Oak.'

Lyle nodded.

Eccles continued, 'From what I've already learned, he seemed to spend most of his time at the hotel. Here to sleep, during the day. And to tend his Buff Orpingtons. But most of the time at the Thatched Oak.'

Moody looked uncertain, then asked, 'Do we take it on, sir?'

'Take it on?' This time Lyle looked puzzled.

'This one.' Moody eyed the room with open distaste. 'Hardy's killing, along with the Wardle killing. If you think they're both connected.'

'They might be,' said Lyle warily.

'In that case . . .'

147

'Inspector Eccles,' Lyle turned to the Detective Inspector. 'This case – this particular killing – is your personal baby . . . am I right?'

'Uhuh.' Eccles nodded.

'Who's idea was it to notify me?'

'That was the ACC's instruction sir. I notified him, and he told me to let you know. I rang the Thatched Oak. They told me you were dining with Sergeant Moody. It seemed right to ask you both to attend.'

'But not that I should take over this case?'

'Not in as many words.' Eccles looked undecided. 'Not a specific instruction to hand the enquiry over to you.'

Moody said, 'I think we should, sir.'

'You,' agreed Lyle. 'You're part of the Calfordshire force. I'm not. I'm here to sort out the Wardle killing . . . not this one.'

Eccles asked, 'So you *don't* think there's a connection?'

'Oh, I do. I'm no great believer in this much of a coincidence. But on the face of things, it *is* a separate crime.'

There was a silence. Eccles and Moody waited. They both looked vaguely sad.

It might have been an impasse, but the door of the cottage opened and a man who was a stranger to Lyle entered and greeted both Eccles and Moody. Eccles did the introductions.

'Adam, this is Detective Superintendent Lyle. Mr Lyle, this is Inspector Suchet.'

As they shook hands, Lyle said, 'Scene of the Crime Officer?'

Suchet nodded, and returned with, 'The man brought in to show us how it should be done?'

'Something along those lines,' agreed Lyle.

'This one, too?' asked Suchet.

'This one . . . maybe,' said Lyle teasingly.

'I like to know who I'm working for,' said Suchet.

'You're working for yourself,' said Lyle mischievously. 'For the loot and all the things the loot can buy. Kid yourself you're working for anything else – for *anybody* else – and you're lying in your own teeth.'

148

'You know what I mean.'

Suchet looked taken aback by Lyle's attitude. It quietened him and, at the same time, brought the flicker of quick smiles to the faces of Eccles and Moody.

Lyle said, 'The body is in the hen house. Take your cellophane envelopes and collect a few droppings. Meanwhile, I'll check. I'll ring the ACC.'

10.00 a.m.

A new day – a miserable, lowering day with an overcast sky heavy with held-back rain . . . and a new murder. It was a grey day, and the colour matched Lyle's mood.

Needham had seemed almost surprised that telephone confirmation had been needed before Lyle took over responsibility for the second murder.

'You're there, Superintendent. You're on the spot. Who else should handle the enquiry?'

Lyle had warned. 'There might *not* be a connection.'

'And if there is? And the chances are there is . . . and you're not in charge?'

'So?' Lyle hadn't sounded too enthusiastic. 'I make it a double-header?'

'Lyle, you do that. As a personal favour. I'll put my authority in writing, if that's what you want. Anything! Just sort out this Gauntley shambles. Name the bastard who thinks he can get away with this sort of caper in this police area.'

And Moody had seemed delighted as, indeed, had Eccles. Suchet had muttered something about the lost delights of working with Hunt, but nobody had taken too much notice of Suchet.

Thereafter, the night had taken on the aspect of routine, and sometimes unutterably boring police work. The occupants of the other three railway cottages had been carefully questioned. Had they heard anything? Had they seen anything? Did they suspect anything? Had anybody told them anything? The questions had been asked, the replies had been noted on forms attached to clipboards. Statements had been taken. More, and back-up, statements had been taken. Even more, and negative, statements had been taken.

As one elderly uniformed copper who was being kept from his bed had put it, 'Much more bloody paperwork, and they'll have to start on another Amazonian rain forest.'

Moody had snatched a few minutes freedom to return to the Thatched Oak and escort his lady love back to her home. Thereafter Moody had tried to be everywhere at the same time. This was, it seemed, a killing he was more than a little eager to solve; a more personal affair than the Wardle killing had been; a butchery which had been virtually committed within the few short minutes when he and Lyle had allowed their attention to wander to more pleasant things. An affront. An insult. A second murder . . . but also an outrage.

Suchet had spent the night putting bits and pieces into tiny envelopes. Droppings from the Buff Orpingtons. Samples from the feed bins. Scrapings from the floors of the hen huts. Samples of earth from the soil around the huts. His tiny penknife had been forever scratching and digging. His supply of self-adhesive labels had been ever-lastingly written upon and carefully affixed. He had worked as hard as any other officer present, if only in justifying his own existence.

Eccles had been the field commander. He'd been the link between Lyle and the actual grass-roots graft. Lyle had remained in Hardy's cottage, while Eccles had gathered together the increasing threads of 'initial action' and repor-ted the results to the Detective Superintendent.

The Photography Section of the force had attended and aimed lenses and exploded flash bulbs with all the enthusi-asm of camera buffs not accountable for the costs of film and equipment.

The Plan Drawing Section had arrived, then having arrived, hadn't been too certain of their place in the scheme of things. To measure. To draw. To counter any inadver-tent inaccuracies suggested by mere photographs.

They had, of course, been mocked.

'Does it matter? To the nearest half-inch? How does the exact position of his left boot help?

'The judge might want the jury to know.'

'Holy cow!'

'They ask these things. Judges. Who the hell knows *what* they might want to know.'

The Dog Section also arrived when every other copper at the scene had figured that the 'specialised services' had cleared the far horizon. They arrived well after midnight.

Nobody had been more outraged than Eccles. 'Who the steaming Christ called *them* out?'

A sergeant dog handler had glared, and said, 'Whoever did it left the scene.'

'The scene's thick in chicken shit. That's about all we're short on – a few piles of dog shit.'

'The dogs might be able to—'

'Keep those damned animals in the shooting brakes. Dogs! Some prize pillock will yell for the Mounted Section next. Let's have a few horses to complete the shambles.'

It had, Lyle decided, been one of those nights. A typical first night overture to a murder enquiry. Everybody doing too much, because everybody was terrified of not doing enough. Too many coppers. Too many 'experts'. Too many pointless questions asked. Too many useless statements taken.

And, of course, the media had been sniffing around. A highly articulate creep from Calfordshire Air Waves and a nondescript sniffler called Logan from the local press. They'd arrived at about dawn, and in the privacy of the dead man's cottage, they'd thrown questions at Lyle, and Lyle – probably because it had been a long, boring and monumentally tiring night – had said things he maybe shouldn't have said; mouthed opinions with a certain directness which suggested that they were more-or-less established facts.

'The usual thing?' William Francis had made it sound like an innocent, throw-away question.

Lyle had looked at him questioningly.

'The usual garbage,' Francis had expanded. ' "Promising enquiries". All that crap?'

'Oh more than "promising enquiries".'

'Oh!'

'We *know*.'

'Ah!'

'*I* know,' Lyle had corrected himself. He'd continued, 'Of course the killer doesn't know I know. Doesn't even guess I know.'

Francis checked that the tape-recorder was switched to record. Logan scribbled like crazy and tried to get it down verbatim.

Lyle went on, 'A couple of days. Maybe less. Just a touch more evidence, then there'll be an arrest.'

'One man?' asked Francis.

'One person,' agreed Lyle.

'And you know who it is?'

'Oh, yes.' Lyle nodded.

'Can we ask?' Francis was bordering upon breathlessness.

'You won't be told,' Lyle had smiled.

'But there's no doubt?'

'Not a scrap of doubt.'

'And – y'know – this is *on* the record?'

'Why not? I haven't disclosed names. The killer feels quite safe.'

'And he's not?'

'That, ' chuckled Lyle, 'is an understatement.'

And that had been it. A recorded conversation which had taken place at about dawn. A smart-cookie of a radio reporter, a slightly dopey newspaperman and a senior police officer who should have known better. And, of course, a round-eyed listening public who'd heard Lyle's confident boast that he knew the identity of his quarry.

And now it was mid-morning and Lyle was waiting in the ante-room of Needham's office, having been instructed to report there, full throttle and without argument, and meanwhile to keep well away from media people, and above all keep his lips closed and his teeth clenched.

152

Interlude

Interlude

The murderer heard the broadcast at eight o'clock, on the hourly news update sent out by Calfordshire Air Waves. It arrived via a transistor radio. It accompanied a snack of instant coffee, a biscuit and a morning cigarette.

Bluff. So thought the murderer. That was the first reaction. A ridiculous, not to say childish, ploy. Meant to induce panic. Meant to play upon the nerves of somebody Lyle had not yet identified. Meant to be a silly, impossible bluff.

Then the murderer had second thoughts.

A superintendent. A high-ranking police officer. A man with brains. Above all a man who, supposedly, dealt only with facts and with evidence.

A man not given to fanciful brainwaves. A man not required to fall back on involved bluff.

The murderer had second thoughts to the second thoughts.

The biscuit was finished. The coffee was drained. The cigarette was squashed into an ash-tray.

The murderer had second thoughts to those second, second thoughts.

The murderer muttered, 'You bastard, you absolute bastard!'

PART FOUR
Lyle's Conclusion

I

I drove back from Calfordshire County Constabulary Headquarters at a very moderate speed. I was lucky and I was very much aware of my luck. Needham had been remarkably understanding . . . which was something new for an Assistant Chief Constable.

'It's not a wise policy, Lyle. I think you should have asked first.'

I'd let the observation ride without comment. I wasn't there to argue. I wasn't going to argue.

Instead of arguing, I asked for certain things; not important things – not things capable of being misconstrued as a deliberate fix – but nevertheless things which only Needham could arrange.

And Needham agreed because Needham, too, wanted this kill-crazy character rounded up and taken out of circulation.

That's what it had been all about, and what it was still all about . . . and Needham had the common gumption to realise that.

Nevertheless, and if only because a sleepless night makes for a certain lack of concentration, I drove carefully and at a very moderate speed.

I made for Easedale and an appointment I'd fixed up while still at force headquarters with Sergeant Poole. I needed to see Poole at least one more time. Questions had not yet been answered, and moreover some of the answers given remained a little strange and unsatisfactory.

As I approached Beechwood Brook I passed Eccles driving towards Calford. The car was one of those low slung, sports jobs. It was painted as near to British racing green as to make no matter, and its twin exhausts gave warning that, whatever else, it was a noisy brute. The car stood out and was easy to spot, which was okay. Mine didn't, and the chances were that Eccles hadn't noticed me in the general stream of traffic.

I drove carefully and at a moderate speed. This, I think, was symptomatic; from now on everything had to be handled with great care . . . and no rush.

II

We were in Poole's own office – the office shared by Poole and Backhouse as section sergeants – and maybe because of this Poole seemed to be more at ease than he'd been when I'd last interviewed him. There was also a simple, one-to-one relationship. Nobody was playing witness-cum-recorder of what we each said.

Poole said, 'There's not much more to tell you, sir. I was with Wardle when we found the body . . . the body of his wife.'

'That word "found".' I sucked my teeth, meditatively. 'It's slightly out of plumb, surely. You didn't "find" as much as "sought".'

'Sir?' He looked puzzled.

'Had the body been on the road.' I waved my hands a little in order to keep my meaning tidy and understandable. 'Had it been on the road,' I repeated, 'it might have been easier to believe. The body in the gutter, say. In the hedge bottom. There . . . in the headlights. But it wasn't. It was away from the road. In a field. And, moreover, the road itself wasn't the sort of road normally patrolled by the police. You didn't *find* the body, Sergeant. You damn near *looked* for it.'

'Sir, that is a deliberate misinterpretation.'

'Not deliberate. A natural interpretation. A two-and-two-make-four interpretation. The sort of interpretation any reasonable man – any reasonable jury – might make. What the hell else, Sergeant? That Hangman's Lane place. It seems to be very appropriately named.'

160

'Sir,' he growled, 'I heard your broadcast earlier this morning.'

'So?'

'You claim to know who the murderer is.'

'I know,' I said in a low voice.

'Me? You think it's *me?*'

'Would I tell you?' I teased.

'You'd be wrong. Monumentally wrong.'

'And if it *is* you, would *you* say anything else?'

'Devious.' He allowed his lips to twist into a quick and crooked smile. 'Very devious, sir.'

'We aren't playing parlour games, Sergeant Poole.'

'I'm not. I don't have to lie, and as long as I stick to the truth—'

'Ah, but you don't,' I cut in. 'You haven't. You've lied already.'

His eyes narrowed a little; part worry, part suspicion. I could almost see the wheels of his mind spinning around, working out the various has-and-has-not remarks already made; fishing around for some word – some phrase – not strictly accurate.

'The Carlton Bingo Hall kiosk,' I murmured.

'I – er – I know it. What about it?'

'That's not where you telephoned in. The night of Mrs Wardle's murder – when you rang this office to say you were going out to Gauntley . . . but not from that kiosk.'

'From that kiosk,' he insisted.

'This nick,' I said quietly. 'It's on the way. From that kiosk going out to Gauntley . . . you *pass* this police station. No need to phone. Why waste time telephoning? Why not just call in while passing?'

I waited. Years of interviewing helped me to make an educated guess as to his reason for not answering immediately. He was collecting his thoughts – choosing the right words before speaking them, but whether those words were going to be gold or garbage had yet to be decided. Therefore I waited; like a prize-fighter waits for the potential knock-out punch to be thrown, knowing he has to slip it, counter it, ride it or hit the canvas. It was a

161

strange feeling. A feeling of exhilaration, coupled with something not far from trepidation. Within the next few moments, Poole's name would either leave the frame or start flashing like Blackpool Illuminations. He started with a question.

'Have you met Constable Boyle?'

I nodded and continued to wait.

'Constable Boyle.' He repeated the name, and the ghost of a grin touched his mouth. 'You see, sir. I suffer from a guts ailment called diverticulitis. That's what the doc tells me. Maybe. Maybe ulcers. Either way it can be painful, and it gets particularly painful when hassle starts. When somebody pushes the panic button. In my own way – on my own – I can cope. I can handle most things.

'Boyle *makes* trouble. A nothing – a simple, everyday incident – and Boyle makes a West End production out of it. Always. He gathers things – collects things – and waits for an opportunity. Then he throws them at you in a stupid, mixed-up exaggeration. He should never have been a copper. He's too unstable. He's the sort of man to whom calmness is a minor blasphemy. He literally invents problems, but without realising he's doing it.'

'And you didn't want to call in at the nick?' I nodded my understanding.

'I already had a mild belly-ache,' he said simply. 'What I *didn't* want, until my guts had straightened themselves out, was Boyle.'

It was such an honest explanation – such a simple explanation – it had to be true. More than that. It sounded true. Because like an off-key note to somebody with perfect pitch, an untruth – even a tiny, unimportant untruth – imposes a discordant obstruction to complete belief in the mind of men whose profession it is to seek out accuracy.

We talked for perhaps another half an hour. No more. What little doubt I'd had about Poole had vanished. He was it seemed, an ordinary man with an ordinary man's weaknesses. It was arguable that his natural disposition was not that of the perfect policeman, but what did that

162

matter? Maybe he worried too much. Maybe he was too prone to carry unnecessary burdens of responsibility. Indeed, maybe he was too nice a guy to be a truly efficient copper.

On the other hand . . .

With all his faults, it could be that Poole was a more complete man than myself.

III

As I climbed from the car and neared the cottage, the feeling touched me. I'd noticed it during the night and what I felt was merely a restatement of a long-held opinion. Where Hardy had once lived now had that cold, clammy feel of a death house.

It happens.

An ordinary death – a natural death, a decent family bereavement – and there is expected sadness. There is a gap, a vacuum, where there had once been life. The stones weep a little, and for a while happiness is absent.

But a violent death – a murder – brings something far different. It is reflected in the very structure and material of the building. And it stays. Such houses are often difficult to sell on the open market. They seem to carry their own peculiar curse; they are haunted by something which has to do with the ripping away of human life. There seems to be a chill, and shadows where there should not be shadows.

I had the feel that Hardy's cottage was already like that.

Moody was waiting at the open door. He'd slipped home for a shower and change of clothes while I'd been away. Now he stood at the open door, and as I moved to within hearshot he spoke.

'Boothroyd,' he growled.

'Eh?' I blinked non-understanding.

'A buddy of Hardy's. Like Hardy, he works at the Thatched Oak. In the kitchens. Scrubbing the pans. That sort of stuff.'

163

'Bully for Boothroyd. Now put me out of my misery. Who the hell *is* Boothroyd?'

'The flasher. Hangman's Lane. Wardle had had him in court the day before his wife was murdered.'

'Boothroyd.' I nodded. 'Right. Now I place him. And you say, what?'

'A friend of Hardy. They both worked at the Thatched Oak. They were friends. That's the link.'

'The link?'

'Between the killings.'

'Oh, for Christ's sake!'

'You said there was a link.' Moody's tone was bordering upon spoiled child petulance. 'Yesterday, when we first arrived here, you said there *was* a connection.'

'It seemed possible,' I admitted. 'Even probable. But – good God, Sergeant – this is a village. A particularly small village. The Thatched Oak. They employ people from the village. And why not? It happens. Often. Any other village, a similar situation—'

'I thought we were looking for a connection.' His tone was distinctly surly. 'I thought that was what you—'

'All right.' I waved a hand. 'Boothroyd – whoever the hell he is – we'll give him a quick going over. Just to be sure.'

IV

And we did. Just 'to be sure' . . . and this despite the fact that I *was* sure already.

It was late morning and the pans and dishes in the kitchen of the Thatched Oak were not yet in need of their daily scouring. Boothroyd was still at his home, and to him and his equally disgusting mother 'home' was what was locally known as a 'low decker' about a hundred yards from what could be taken as the edge of the village.

It stood at one corner of a field, with a tiny wood along one side of the badly tended garden. Moss was growing between the roof slabs. The woodwork was screaming for

164

a coat of paint. The windows were dirty and the curtains were tatty. It was the definitive rural slum.

Inside the main room stank of cats and worse. Dirty crockery stood on a stained table in the middle of the room. Boothroyd, wearing ancient corduroy trousers with the braces over a soiled sweat-shirt, sat in a broken-springed armchair and reluctantly answered our questions.

His disgusting mother stood, arms folded, on the clipped rug in front of a dead hearth. She might have been the Earth Mother protecting her young ... except that now and again her tone and her words suggested that she held her offspring in even more scorn than we did.

'You know Hangman's Lane,' I said.

'Who doesn't?'

'I didn't,' I countered. 'But I know it now. It's where the Wardle killing took place. It's where you exposed yourself.'

'I paid the sodding fine,' he growled.

'For what good *that* does,' observed Moody.

The mother said, 'He didn't hurt anybody.'

'I didn't hurt anybody,' echoed Boothroyd.

'And that excuses everything?' Moody's voice was ugly with contempt. 'Pissing in the street, emptying your bowels behind somebody's garden wall ... *that* doesn't hurt anybody. But—'

'You knew Constable Wardle,' I interrupted. 'Knew him. Didn't like him.'

'Knew him. *Know* him.' The contempt matched Moody's. 'Hated him. *Still* hate him.'

'For doing his job?'

The mother said, 'He was only doing his job.'

'Hate him enough to murder him?' I asked. 'Hated him enough to murder his wife?'

'Don't pin that thing on me!'

The mother began, 'Hey—'

'Shut it!' I rounded on her. 'Let the animal give his own answers.' Then to Boothroyd, 'Enough to murder his wife? Enough to boast about it where you work at the

Thatched Oak? Get drunk, maybe? Tell your pal, Hardy? Then when you'd sobered up, realised what you'd done. Then, of course, you'd have to strangle Hardy to keep him quiet. It's so bloody obvious. You don't even need pencil and paper.'

'No, I – no, I . . .'

The mother breathed, 'He wouldn't have the balls.'

'And you should know!' He rounded on her and spat his loathing into her face. He turned to me and snarled, 'Look, copper. Last time I saw Oliver was in the Oak's kitchen. Yesterday afternoon. Check up. Ask. They'll tell you.'

Moody snapped, 'We will. And they'd better.'

'He left to feed his hens. He didn't come back. Next I knew, he'd been found dead. In the hen house . . . that's what they say.'

'It's the truth,' I murmured.

'And me? I never left the Oak. Never left the kitchen. The kitchen staff'll tell you. All that scrubbing and swilling. Why the hell they can't—'

'Not him,' the mother interrupted. 'Not *him*. All *he's* good for is shoving his hands in hot soapy water. That's all *he's* good for.'

'Leave it, woman,' I rasped. I flicked my eyes around the room and added, 'Hot soapy water might not do too much harm in this place.'

And that was it. That was all it could ever be.

We played games for another half hour or so. Calling Boothroyd a liar. Setting simple traps with our questions, and watching him blindly stumble into them. The mother despised the son and the son scorned the mother. Moody did nothing to hide his utter disparagement for the pair of them. As for myself . . . it was, I suppose, an exercise in open derision. Such people are not to be thought of as pathetic; pathos equates with sympathy and sorrow. But the Boothroyds of the world are merely disgusting.

It was, as I say, an exercise. A warming-up. A getting-going and a final polishing of whatever technique I possessed for teasing the truth from its hiding place.

166

V

Eccles was waiting for us at the Hardy cottage. The afternoon had just started and a lunch break wasn't too far away. As Moody and I entered the cottage, I saw the gun. It was an old World War II handgun, favoured by the German army. A Walther P38.

Never a beautiful gun – never even a finely-finished gun – it nevertheless looked both dirty and deadly as it claimed centre stage on the table.

Eccles flicked a finger and said, 'Upstairs. Behind the wardrobe.'

'We find them,' I observed grimly. 'Everybody feels big with a shooter in the house. Why in hell we bother with the occasional amnesty. The idiots still keep guns hidden away in drawers . . . or behind wardrobes.'

Moody asked, 'Is it loaded?'

I lifted the pistol from the table, cocked it, checked that the safety catch was off, then tilted the barrel and squeezed the trigger. The gun bucked slightly in my hand as the cartridge exploded and the 9mm slug smacked itself into the soil of the nearby railway embankment.

'Now we know,' I murmured. I thumbed down the safety catch and handed the pistol to Moody. 'Take care of it until we get back to Easedale. Then bung it into a safe, pending it being handed over to the ballistics boys.'

Moody took the offered gun.

'Shouldn't we—' began Eccles.

'I'm not going near Easedale,' I interrupted. 'Neither are you until much later. I'd like a council of war this evening. You, me and Suchet. Needham is demanding certain answers. And fast.'

'Er, this morning . . .' Eccles looked a little embarrassed. 'On the local radio.'

'I know.' I nodded. 'Needham heard it, too.'

'You weren't – y'know – serious?'

'I was serious,' I assured him.

'You *know*?' This time Moody looked a mite dumbfounded.

167

'I don't make wild statements, Sergeant. Especially when there's every likelihood that what I say is going to be made public.'

'In that case, why not . . .'

'Sergeant . . .' I compressed my lips and shook my head in mild disapproval. 'Put yourself in the murderer's shoes. To know that *I* know and to be helpless. To expect to be arrested. Charged. Hopefully, convicted. Very off-putting . . . wouldn't you say? Very panic-causing. It makes for sleepless nights.'

Moody looked uncertain, then said, 'It also puts him on his guard.'

'Does it?'

'That's what I would think.'

'The obvious opinion. The fictional opinion.' I treated him to a quick, knowing smile. 'The denouement crap. All the suspects in one room. The great detective doing his party piece. Yards of time-wasting while he plays out his elimination game. Then the great unmasking.' I sent him another quick smile, then asked, 'Do you think that, Sergeant? Do you really think *that?*'

'It puts him on his guard,' he repeated.

'No.' This time I chuckled. 'The mistakes have already been made. They can't be unmade. They can't even be covered up.'

Eccles said, 'I think I'm with Moody, sir.'

'In that case you're wrong too. After this morning the murderer *knows* I know. He can't kid himself any longer. By this time tomorrow he'll be tucked away in a police cell. He knows that, too. There are few certainties in life, Inspector, but the murderer can count on that one. He'll be banged up by morning.'

I think both Eccles and Moody counted me at least foolish. Maybe a braggart. Maybe both. The subject was dropped, and after checking that the cottage was secure and ready for our return, we retired for lunch – my treat – to the Thatched Oak.

168

The waiter was still in attendance. He handed out the menu cards, then left us.

I said, 'We've all three had a long night. Done without both supper and breakfast. Let's relax a little and for a change concentrate our attention on the inner man.'

The other two nodded and grunted agreement, then began to scan the menu on offer.

For starters I chose potted shrimps. The other two chose melon. As we waited, we sipped Muscadet Sevre et Maine, chosen by me because of its dryness and because of its remarkably gentle strength.

'I met Sergeant Moody's future wife last night.' I spoke to Eccles. 'Susan. A remarkable young lady.'

Moody grinned his approval of the assessment.

'Remarkable?' Eccles didn't sound too sure of my meaning.

'Good looking,' I explained.

'Oh!'

'Very much in command.'

'Ah!'

'I really can't see the good sergeant misbehaving himself, once the knot's tied,' I murmured.

'Nor would he want to,' smiled Moody.

'Not at first,' agreed Eccles. 'They never do . . . at first.'

'I don't see how . . .' began Moody. But the waiter arrived with the shrimps and the melons, and I raised one hand a few inches from the surface of the table in order to suggest that the talk, the discussion, the leg-pulling might be postponed until he was out of earshot.

The waiter asked, 'Everything to your satisfaction, sir?'

'Oh, I think things are lining up very promisingly, don't you, Inspector?'

Eccles nodded and smiled, 'With luck. With a certain amount of luck . . . hopefully, that is.'

'What?' Moody looked puzzled.

'Sergeant?' I asked.

'I don't know what . . .'

'Are you *satisfied*?' I amplified.

'Oh – er – yes.'

'With the melon?'

'Yes. Yes . . . of course.'

'With everything?'

'Yes, sir. Certainly. With everything.'

'That makes me happy,' I assured him. 'That makes me very happy.' I turned to the waiter, and said, 'Detective Sergeant Moody is satisfied with everything.'

'Yes, sir. I'm glad.'

'Good.' A carefully timed pause. As the waiter turned to leave the table, I added, 'You knew the late Mr Hardy, of course.'

'Oh, yes. Yes, sir. We all knew Mr Hardy.' The waiter paused and turned back towards the table. 'Why do you ask, sir?'

'He's dead.' I drained my glass, then added, 'You'll know that, I suppose?'

'Oh, yes. We know he's dead.'

'Murdered.'

'Yes, sir.'

'Do you miss him?' asked Eccles.

'Personally?'

'Personally. Generally. Whichever way you wish. Do you miss him?'

'We haven't yet had time,' fenced the waiter.

'You'll be sending a wreath?' suggested Eccles.

'Not personally, sir. I expect there'll be a whip-round.'

'I can't see what—' began Moody.

'You didn't even like him enough to send a personal wreath?' I teased.

'No, sir.' The waiter hesitated, then added, 'I don't think anybody liked him enough for that.'

'Look—' Moody tried again.

'Sergeant,' I explained. 'To us – to you and me and Inspector Eccles – Hardy is merely a corpse. The end product of manual strangulation. But to his workmates . . .'

'I wouldn't call him that, sir,' objected the waiter.

Eccles came in with, 'He worked here.'

170

'Quite so, sir. But he had few friends at the Thatched Oak.'

'And why was that?' I asked.

'He could never keep his own council.'

'Really?' I smiled.

Eccles said, 'You surprise us, young man.'

'Do I?' The waiter allowed himself the luxury of a very knowing smile and repeated, 'Do I really, sir?' then soft-footed his way across the room and through the door to the kitchens.

We finished what was left of the shrimps and melons and waited. Other than our table the room was empty. Clean white cloths covered the tops of the tables. Identical cruet sets stood in the geometrical centre of each cloth. Chairs were pushed in around each table. The long, dark sideboard was bare except for about half-a-dozen bottles occupying the giant-sized rack which made up its middle section. The carpet of the room was newly Hoovered and crumbless.

As I lighted a cigarette, I glanced around the room, took in the details and remarked, 'A nice place. Well above average.'

'It's nice.' Moody agreed with me. It sounded a little like a hurried agreement. As if he figured it was time he said something. As if he'd been silent for too long.

Eccles asked, 'Do you come here often, then?'

'Occasionally.'

'With Susan?' I asked.

'She likes the food here.'

'With other people?'

'I – er – I guess. Sometimes.'

'Pricey for a detective sergeant,' observed Eccles.

'Not really.'

'No?'

'I'm not married.'

'Yet,' I murmured.

Moody blinked, but closed his mouth.

Moody was getting the message. We were ganging up on him. And it was more than teasing. More than leg-pulling.

171

Far more. In its own way it was hurtful and, moreover, it was meant to be hurtful.

Eccles said, 'You enjoyed the melon, Sergeant?'

'Of course.'

'Good.'

'Why? Why do you ask?'

'The condemned man,' smiled Eccles . . . but there was nothing humorous about the smile.

'The *what!*'

'Condemned man,' I explained. 'You're on the point of getting married, aren't you?'

'Oh!' But Moody's eyes didn't smile. They were angry, but they were also worried. Maybe even scared.

A waitress came and cleared away the used crockery and cutlery. Our friend the waiter arrived with the main course. Grilled fillet steak for myself. Lamb cutlets for the other two. The vegetables, the potatoes, the mushrooms and the sauted onions were plentiful and the waiter served and set the table with a deftness which only years of practice brings.

He folded a napkin around the bottle and topped up our glasses. Then he stood to one side. Feet close together. Legs stiff. Body bent a little forward. Arms straight and hands clasped behind his back. It was a strangely Spanish posture.

'Mint sauce?' he asked.

'No, thank you.'

'Mustard, perhaps?'

'No, thank you.'

'Anything else at all, gentlemen?'

Eccles said, 'A few answers.'

'Answers?'

'To questions,' I echoed.

'Sir?'

'Questions about, say, Tabitha Wardle.' Eccles and I took it in turns to fire the questions.

The waiter said, 'Ah!' and looked worried.

'Her paramours,' I murmured.

'Ah!'

'Plural,' said Eccles softly.

'Sir, I—'

172

'Which bedroom?' I asked.

'Sir, I—'

'For Christ's sake, don't be coy.'

'It – er . . .'

'Nature intended it to be so,' I encouraged.

'Yes, sir. But—'

'This is where she humped,' said Eccles flatly. 'You're not telling *us*. We're telling *you*. Now . . . which was her favourite bedroom?'

'I don't – I don't . . .'

'You bloody-well *do*,' I snapped.

'Sir.' The waiter swallowed. 'It's not my business.'

'No?'

'It's – it's not . . .'

'It's your business,' snarled Eccles. 'It's *our* business, and we're asking questions. You're here to answer them. That makes it *your* business.'

'Sir, I don't think I should—'

'Here or at the nick.' I tightened the screw. 'You owe a loyalty to this place – to the Thatched Oak. Great. If you think that loyalty includes being charged with obstructing the police – and in a murder enquiry – go right ahead. Just so that you know where you stand. What's going to happen. That's all.'

'Sir, it was . . .' He swallowed, then muttered, 'It was usually Room Seventeen. That's what I'm told. The use of Room Seventeen.'

'First floor?' I asked.

'Ground floor, sir.' He sighed, as if in final resignation. 'It – er – it's easily accessible. As if – y'know – as if you're going to the toilets. But turn right along the corridor immediately beyond the toilets. On the left. The linen room. The cleaners' store. Then Room Seventeen.'

'There we are. It wasn't too painful, was it?' I mocked.

Eccles said, 'The details, if you please, young man.'

'I think . . .' The waiter moistened his lips. 'I'm not sure about this, but I think she slipped the receptionist – maybe the night porter – a fiver for the use of the room for an hour or so. I *think* that's how it was worked.'

173

'And the manager?' I asked.

'He knew nothing. I'm sure of that. Nothing at all. He'd have . . .' He flapped his arms, penguin-style, as he sought the right words.

'And who can blame him?' I murmured.

VII

Room Seventeen.

We'd finished the meal. The lamb cutlets. The grilled steak. The vegetables and the trimmings. Thereafter the cream gateaux and the two portions of apple pie. And finally the coffee, cheese and biscuits.

We'd smoked cigarettes. We'd let the waiter off the hook, and Moody had regained some of his composure.

Then, with no rush whatever, we'd made our way through the rooms and corridors of the ground floor to Room Seventeen.

It was not much different from the room I was occupying. Maybe a little larger. En suite bathroom, complete with thick, white towels. Tea-making equipment. Electric trouser press. A neatly made double bed. A couple of wardrobes. A chest of drawers. A dressing table. Table-lamps, a telephone, bedside tables. The usual moderately top line hotel.

Moody looked around the room, then said, 'Very comfortable.'

'For what Tabitha Wardle used for it,' agreed Eccles.

I lowered myself onto the edge of the bed, and said, 'Shall we cut the crap? Shall we examine the facts? Then reach certain conclusions?'

Eccles said, 'I thought we knew the facts.' He lowered himself onto one of the chairs. 'I thought we'd known the facts about the Wardle woman for some time.'

'She hawked herself,' said Moody. He moved, and stood with his back to the window. He added, 'That seems to be the general impression . . . regardless of how much Constable Wardle doesn't like the sound of it.'

'She wasn't murdered because she hawked herself,' I said gently.

'Indirectly?' suggested Moody.

' "Yorkshire Ripper" indirectly,' teased Eccles. 'Shifting immorality, tart at a time, and who cares if some of 'em *aren't* tarts?'

'No. Not that?'

'Not that,' I agreed. 'Otherwise, it makes the killer as mad as a hatter. And whatever else, not that.'

'Not mad?' Moody made it a half-question.

'No more than all killers are mad.' Eccles provided a decent answer.

Outside it had begun to rain. Gusts of wind sent drops onto the glass behind Moody.

'She was killed,' I said, 'because she was too obliging with her favours. Because she wasn't discreet enough. She might have talked. Told the wrong people.'

'And that,' said Eccles, 'makes our killer a man. That's detection for you, Sergeant. One conclusion, and half the world's population is immediately eliminated.'

Eccles chuckled at his non-joke. Moody frowned a vague puzzlement. I kept straight-faced.

I said, 'Let's go back to basics.' I turned to Eccles. 'You were notified of Wardle's murder . . . when?'

'About four – five to, five past – somewhere between those times. The early hours of August first.'

'And you?' I looked at Moody.

'At about the same time. I – er – I don't know who they telephoned first, but they notified us both at the same time.'

'Good. Good.' I gave a couple of slow nods. Solemn, ponderous nods. As if some very involved equation had gradually resolved itself. I said, 'You were both in bed at that time, right?'

'Yes.'

'Of course. At that hour.'

'You would be.' A quicker nod, as an appreciation of my supposition being verified. I added, 'At that hour, of course you would be.'

175

Eccles said, 'For myself, I dressed. Splashed water onto my face and went downstairs to wait for the Sergeant here.'

'A long wait?' I asked.

'No wait at all. I was in the kitchen – I'd popped in, with the hope of a quick brew-up – when he arrived.'

'No brew-up?'

'No.' Eccles gave a quick grin. 'Chop-chop. I had no way of knowing whether Hunt would be at the scene.'

'That man,' I said dreamily. 'If *I* had that effect upon people . . .'

'I heard the Sergeant sound his horn, so I didn't even switch the kettle on. Out and away. Like a pair of dutiful jacks.'

'That,' added Moody, 'was the effect Hunt had on everybody.'

He had a slightly vague smile on his lips. Vague. A little worried. Like a man not quite as sure of himself as he thought he was.

'You drove straight to Beechwood Brook having received the call?'

'Oh yes, sir. As soon as I'd put the phone down.'

'You dressed, of course?'

'Yes. Naturally.'

'But no meal? No quick snack.'

'No time, sir.'

'Just out of bed, into some clothes and into the car.'

'That's about it, sir.'

'Odd.' I did a slow, chin-rubbing routine, then muttered, 'I find that very strange.'

He looked a little less vague. A little more worried.

'You get my meaning,' I murmured.

'Well, to be honest, sir. No. I can't see what . . .'

'Ten miles,' I reminded him. 'Ten miles . . . that equates with ten minutes. At least ten minutes. Even if the roads were empty. Even if you had your foot down every inch of the way. *And* in the wrong direction.'

'Sir, I'm sorry. I still don't . . .'

'Inspector Eccles has to get dressed. You, too – out of bed then get dressed. About the same time. Not more than

176

a minute – two minutes – in the time it takes.'

'Sir, I . . .'

'Item: the telephone bell awakens you. Item: you answer it.' It was a little like rocking an impossibly heavy rock in the hope that, eventually, it would roll and tumble over the lip of a precipice. I continued, 'Item: you get out of bed. Item: you visit the bathroom. Item: you have a quick wash. Item: you dress. Both of you. That's what happens. But you, Sergeant, *you* . . . you also drive a motor car ten miles. Ten miles . . . ten minutes. At least ten minutes. Can we please figure out where those ten minutes went?'

'Ten minutes, sir. That's not much—'

'Ah, but it *is*,' I cut in. 'Ask Charlie Calverley. Ten minutes is a long time . . . it's "forever" if the gags aren't going down. The average time of a music hall turn. Not long if you're measuring in hours. But when you're measuring in *minutes* – like we are – a long time. One hell of a difference between one man jumping out of bed and getting dressed, and another man doing exactly the same thing.' I paused and looked duly puzzled. 'That's all I want, Sergeant. To know how those ten minutes – maybe more, but certainly no less – can be accounted for.'

Moody said, 'Ah!' then closed his mouth and screwed his face into an expression of deep thought. Then his eyes widened and, for a moment, I thought he was going to laugh aloud. 'I have it. Of *course*,' he smiled.

'Share it, please,' I suggested.

'I wasn't *in* bed.' He made a tiny chopping movement with his right hand. 'I'd been with – y'know – Susan.' He looked remarkably sheepish as he continued, 'We'd had quite a session. Snogging. We'd . . . lost count of the time. Sorry. I should have remembered.' He paused, then went on, 'I'd parked the car. I was just going to hang my jacket in the wardrobe. That's when the telephone bell rang.'

'It takes care of the ten minutes,' I admitted. 'The Inspector here was getting up and getting dressed while you drove from Easedale to Beechwood Brook, right?'

'That's it, sir,' he agreed. 'Sorry. I should have remembered.'

VIII

The conversation seemed to have developed a sheen of perspiration. Each word was a droplet of sweat, and the sweat was a sweat of terror. We all three knew. The truth was no longer hidden. It was there, waiting to be dragged into the open; its wicked little eyes gleaming defiance from the hole it had scurried into.

'You forgot?' I murmured.

'Strange, I know.' Moody tried to smile. He almost made it.

'Strange,' I agreed.

Eccles looked both grim and sad. He didn't smile.

'You went to Hangman's Lane,' I said. 'With the Inspector. To Hangman's Lane.'

'To the scene. To Hangman's Lane.'

'And?'

'I did what I could. Which wasn't much. Then Suchet arrived, and I helped him cordon off.'

'The lane?'

Moody nodded.

'Not the body? Not the field?'

'He stayed in the lane,' growled Eccles. 'He didn't go near the body.'

'Agreed?' I asked.

'Mantell was there.'

'So?'

'Christ, *Mantell*.' He gave it as an explanation.

'Inspector Mantell,' said Eccles. 'He goes by the book.'

'He kept everybody clear of the field,' said Moody. 'So scared of doing anything wrong, he did *nothing*.'

'When did you see the body of Tabitha Wardle?' I asked.

'I—'

'Both barrels in the chest,' I teased. 'Remember? Some of the shot went all the way through and broke twigs in the hedge. Remember? All that blood. All that mangled flesh. It made you feel like puking when you only remembered it. Fine . . . remember it *now*.'

'I don't know what you're talking about,' he croaked.

178

But he was lying. Both Eccles and I knew he was lying . . . and he knew we knew.

I was still rocking the impossibly heavy rock. But the rhythm of the rocking was having an effect. The arc of the swing was getting larger, and with each heave the lip of the precipice became a more reasonable goal.

I said, 'Your fiancée – Susan – might have found out. She already had her suspicions.'

'About . . . about what?' It was a dry question, and without either anger or real denial.

'About Mrs Wardle. About Wardle's wife. About the field in Hangman's Lane . . . the field you know so much about.'

'I – I . . .'

'About this room. About the only time you saw Tabitha Wardle, with her guts hanging out.'

'I – I – I . . .'

'About the humping sessions you didn't want Susan to know about. About Hardy knowing – guessing – what went on in this room. About you seeing him talking to me. Telling me. Verifying what I already guessed . . .'

'You can't prove . . . You can't prove a thing. It's all guesswork. And you're wrong. Of course you're wrong.'

'Chicken shit on the Thatched Oak door mat,' I lied. 'And from Buff Orpingtons. Hardy's Buff Orpingtons. From your shoes. Where else? And this room. The bed linen. The carpet. You think Suchet can't come up with something? When he knows where to look and what to look for? You know the police machine better than that, Moody. You know you're cooked, basted, crisp and ready for serving. You, my twisted little friend, are already a tasty meal, waiting to be served with all the trimmings at some future crown court. Hard or easy . . . that's the choice. The *only* choice.'

As I finished speaking I eased open the drawer of the bedside table. At the same time, Moody dipped his hand into his pocket and brought out the Walter P.38. He thumbed the safety catch off, and pointed the snout at a point midway between Eccles and myself.

179

I raised an eyebrow and murmured, 'And what would Susan say about this?'

'Bugger Susan!' Panic, fear and self-disgust mixed with the upsurge of anger. 'And bugger *you*, Lyle.'

'Temper,' I said gently.

'I'll use this thing,' he gabbled. 'Don't think I won't. Make a move to do anything heroic . . . I'll use it. I swear. Both of you.'

'And all for the love of a woman,' mocked Eccles.

'Don't be bloody stupid.' The words, and the expression which accompanied the words were both equally ugly. '*She* wouldn't understand. She asks . . . she gets. There's no give and take in *her* life. She'll – she'll—'

'She'll make somebody a good wife,' I said contemptuously. 'But not you. Not now. Not after you've shot Wardle and strangled Hardy.'

He stared at me. Eyes glaring. Nostrils wide. Mouth slightly slack.

'What was it?' I chuckled. 'Wouldn't she let you have your oats? Is that it? But Tabitha would, and Hardy clicked? And you became scared, scared of sweet little Susan? Scared you wouldn't be sharing all that lovely loot her old man will be pushing in her direction one day?'

'You bastard!' The Walther's tiny black eye stared directly at me, and the knuckle of Moody's trigger-finger showed a slight paleness. He breathed, 'I could kill you, Lyle. Don't think otherwise. You're nothing to me. Nothing!'

'You'd better hope so.' I dropped my hand into the drawer of the bedside table and lifted out the official issue .38 Webley. It was there because it was meant to be there; because Eccles had placed it there after his visit to Needham's office earlier in the day. Just as the Walther had been on Hardy's table, because that, too, had been provided by the force ballistics department. As I weighed the revolver in my hand, I added, 'You're going to have to use that shooter, Moody. And if you're thinking of doing so . . . think ahead a little.'

It was, then, decision time. And Moody couldn't bring

himself to make the decision. His mouth opened and closed, but no words came. His unblinking stare never left my face. The Walther never wavered, but he obviously couldn't bring himself to squeeze the trigger.

I put him out of his misery.

In as calm a voice as I could manage, I said, 'You should know. That pistol you're holding isn't loaded. Cocked, but not loaded. Just the one round in the magazine to make you think it *was* loaded.' I paused, then added, 'You've been conned, Moody. You've been led up the garden path. You're in the fertiliser, friend . . . right up to the neck.'

He didn't quite believe me. He had that shaved splinter of doubt; doubt enough to make him give a quick blink, then squeeze the trigger. The Walther's firing pin fell onto an empty chamber and the gun gave a tiny click. That was all.

I said, 'I could shoot you, Moody. This one *is* loaded. I could put a round into your leg. Your arm. Your guts. I could bloody well kill you . . . and plead that I thought that pistol was loaded. Eccles would back me. In the line of duty. That's what I could claim. And would . . .'

But, I didn't have to go on. Moody had dropped his gaze. He was gaping at the Walther, but not seeing it for the tears streaming from his eyes. The sobs ripped through him and, as Eccles stepped forward to take the Walther and to fasten the handcuffs, he offered no resistance.

IX

Needham looked grimly satisfied. Eccles looked a neat mix of anger and disgust. Me? I don't doubt I looked what I felt. Sad. Maybe even a little miserable.

Needham said, 'We owe you something, Lyle.'

'It came off,' I grunted. I tasted my low alcohol drink, then added, 'He's a weak man. Anybody with character wouldn't have allowed the Morley woman to take over.'

'She's his fiancée.' It was a statement of fact rather than

181

an explanation or an excuse. Needham continued, 'From what I gather, she's a strong willed woman. She's—'

'She keeps her bloody legs crossed,' growled Eccles bluntly. 'That's one reason – maybe the main reason – Moody turned killer.'

I smiled, but without mirth. The last few days had been no joke, and this was no punch line.

Needham and I had eaten a silent, brooding dinner at the Thatched Oak. Good food, wasted. Then we'd retired to the bar, and Eccles had joined us. He'd come from Beechwood Brook where he'd been getting the paperwork under way. Where Moody had had that vital, initial interview and where he'd been locked away in the cells for the night, to live with his own conscience.

Eccles had said, 'He's coughed. By morning, he'll cough a lot more. He's scared out of his wits.'

'With cause,' I'd observed. 'Coppers in prison. It's like throwing a rat into a cage of wild cats.'

'I shouldn't feel sorry,' Needham had scowled. 'I shouldn't . . . but dammit I *do*.'

Me, too. Not sorry, but maybe disappointed. Let down. Figuratively speaking, kicked in the crotch. I wanted out. Away from this God-forsaken constabulary.

I was drinking low alcohol stuff. Eccles was downing gin and orange. Needham stayed with whisky on the rocks.

And now it was goodbye time, and neither the ACC or the DI could fully understand. Questions remained to be answered, but the answers were there if they would only look hard enough.

Needham said, 'You could wait for morning. It's one hell of a time to leave.'

'I need to go. Eccles can build the file for the prosecution. He knows the facts.'

'Why the gun?' muttered Eccles. 'Why *two* guns? If you knew it was Moody, why the involved play-acting?'

'I only thought it was him,' I corrected Eccles. 'Thought it might be him. A gut feeling. His knowledge of Hangman's Lane. The way he couldn't describe Wardle's corpse. The missing ten minutes. The murder of Hardy, almost immediately after Moody had seen him talking to me. All pointers. All nothings. But enough "nothings" to add up to a possible "something".

'Give him the gun. A man with a gun – a man like Moody with a gun – is ten feet tall. Then push him. Mouth him around a little. Twist his brain. Hammer at his emotions. Then if he pulls the gun, give him room to screw himself into the ground.'

'Sly,' muttered Eccles.

'But why two guns?' asked Needham.

'Sir, we're talking about guns.' I tried to hide my impatience. 'We're talking about a murderer with a shooter in his fist. Maybe the gun he's holding isn't loaded . . . even though he thinks it is. On the other hand, as they say, a lot of people have been killed with "unloaded" firearms. Just in case – just in case there'd been a slip-up – I wanted to be able to shoot back.'

And quite suddenly it was all so stupid. Talk of guns. Talk of murder. Talk of the extra suffering of coppers doing time.

I finished my drink, then said, 'I'm on my way, gentlemen.'

'The offer still stands,' said Needham. 'A detective chief superintendentship. No strings. The chair's empty and waiting.'

'Thanks . . . but no thanks.'

Eccles held out his hand, and I shook it. Then Needham, and then I turned on my heels and left. The cases were already packed and waiting by the reception desk; the reception desk which had once been Hardy's special domain.

I didn't ask for help. It needed two journeys, but I carried the cases to the car myself, then left the key on the desk.

Then I wished the Thatched Oak a silent farewell and drove away without even the hint of a regret.

X

What makes Rogate-on-Sands so special? What in hell do I
owe the place? The only thing it has ever given me is
anguish and heartbreak.

And yet . . .

It was a couple of hours past midnight, and the pier was
deserted. I walked slowly to the end and as I walked I
could hear the splash and suck of the waves breaking
against the iron uprights beneath me. I could see the lights
of the prom curving away along the coast. Now and again
the splash of headlights disappearing behind the hide of
Rock Walk. And above the sky was an impossible velvet
blue; a great, navy coloured shroud, with pin-pricks of
stars scattered, like tiny sequins in a massive ball-gown.

I was home. I was tired, but I was clean.

And I decided, Rogate-on-Sands was very special . . .
because it was Rogate-on-Sands.